LOVE AND PROTECT

BOOK ONE IN THE HEROES OF EVERS, TEXAS SERIES

LORI RYAN

D1366683

OTHER BOOKS BY LORI RYAN

The Sutton Billionaires Series:

The Billionaire Deal

Reuniting with the Billionaire

The Billionaire Op

The Billionaire's Rock Star

The Billionaire's Navy SEAL

Falling for the Billionaire's Daughter

The Sutton Capital Intrigue Series:

Cutthroat

Cut and Run

Cut to the Chase

The Sutton Capital on the Line Series:

Pure Vengeance

Latent Danger

The Triple Play Curse Novellas:

Game Changer

Game Maker

Game Clincher

The Heroes of Evers, TX Series:

Love and Protect

Promise and Protect

Honor and Protect (An Evers, TX Novella)

Serve and Protect

Desire and Protect

Cherish and Protect

Treasure and Protect

The Dark Falls, CO Series:

Dark Falls

Dark Burning

Dark Prison

Coming Soon – The Halo Security Series:

Dulce's Defender

Hannah's Hero

Shay's Shelter

Callie's Cover

Grace's Guardian

Sophie's Sentry

Sienna's Sentinal

For the most current list of Lori's books, visit her website: loriryanromance.com.

CHAPTER ONE

L aura Kensington watched the clock on the microwave and willed the phone to ring. Patrick would be home within the hour. If "John Smith" didn't call soon, she'd... Well, she didn't know what she'd do. If he called after six o'clock, she'd have to try to convince Patrick it was a wrong number.

He wouldn't fall for that. Even genuine wrong numbers had gotten her into trouble before.

"Please," she whispered to the phone, her eyes darting toward the front of the house as though she might see him coming any moment. "Just ring, *please.*"

The numbers on the microwave stared back at her, blank and unfeeling. Twelve minutes past five. The clock didn't care that time was running out, that she was cutting this much too close. She wiped the counter down for the tenth time, knowing it would do nothing to still the jittery feel of hands that needed to keep busy, of palms that wouldn't stop sweating.

Forty-eight minutes left. Laura's heart felt as if it would jump out of her chest as she gave in and sat down, then cradled her head in her hands. The phone rang. How was it that a sound she was waiting for—hoping for—sent her into a panic?

"Hello?"

"Mrs. Kensington?" came Smith's voice on the other end. She had talked to him before, but hadn't met with him in person. He sounded kind, even though she knew he was a man who spent a lot of time with unsavory people. But that was to be expected given his profession. Despite that, she'd been told he often worked with women who needed to leave a spouse and who wished not to be found again. Maybe there was an empathetic side to him. Something that touched him and made him want to help women like her get away.

"Yes, speaking."

"Can you talk now?" he asked and she knew right away what he meant. He had never asked why she was leaving and she certainly hadn't volunteered the information, but it seemed as if he knew without having to ask. Just the thought that he knew her secret made her uncomfortable and itchy in her own skin.

"Yes, my husband is still at work, but I don't have long."

"Did you get the first package?" He had mailed it to a post office box she'd set up two towns over from where she and Patrick lived in Windsor, Connecticut.

"Yes, the temporary license and birth certificate."

"Good. You'll be able to use that for a little while, but I need to get you a real birth certificate and social security card if you want to be able to find a job that doesn't pay under the table. That's going to take time."

"How much time?" Laura asked, wanting the answer to be days, not weeks or months, but that was unlikely.

"Not for another few weeks. It takes time to get a real

birth certificate and once that's in place, it takes a little longer for your social security number to come through," he said with the tone of a man who had explained all this to her before. He had. She was partly just nervous and partly hoping for a different answer this time. This just *had* to work. There wasn't any other option.

Before Laura could answer, he continued with instructions. "Save this phone number. I'll need you to call me in three weeks and let me know where you are. I'll need a mailing address." There was no talk of payment. She'd already paid in full just to get him started on the new identity for her. He also didn't ask when she was leaving and she didn't tell him. He seemed to assume she wouldn't be in town in three weeks' time and he was right. Laura would be running next week, as soon as Patrick left on his business trip.

The sound of car tires crunching up the drive sent acid churning through Laura's stomach. She thought she'd be sick, but that wasn't unusual nowadays. She was nauseated for several hours every day and often had to run to the bathroom to be sick.

"I have to go," Laura whispered and didn't wait for a response. She tucked the phone in her pocket and turned to the stove, focusing on making her breathing normal, making sure nothing seemed out of place.

She had laid out every ingredient of the stir-fry she would cook that night for dinner. Everything was diced and chopped and ready to go. Patrick didn't like his dinner to be ready before he arrived home, but he wanted it cooked immediately after his arrival. And, it had better be fast. Laura checked off each ingredient in her mind while she waited for the sound of Patrick's key in the lock.

It didn't come. A moment later the doorbell rang.

Nothing could have prepared Laura for what she saw when she looked through the etched glass panes at the side of the front door.

Police? What are the police doing here?

A scene from two weeks back flashed briefly before her eyes. Her husband taping something to the bottom of one of the kitchen drawers. She'd tried to walk out of the room before he realized she was there, but she'd been too slow to process the scene and move. Patrick wasn't often found in the kitchen and he certainly wouldn't be looking through a drawer. She was responsible for the cooking and cleaning, for putting dishes away. She served his meals in the dining room. Always.

When he'd caught her watching as he taped something to the bottom of the utensil drawer, she'd seen the expected flare of anger in his eyes. But, she'd also seen fear beneath it. And, that was something she'd never seen before. Patrick Kensington feared nothing and no one. In that moment, she'd known her plan to leave had been the right one. It was now or never as Patrick became more unpredictable by the day.

Later, with shaking hands, she'd pulled the drawer out to peer underneath it. A USB drive. The memory of it made her shiver now, as she wrapped her arms around her waist and pulled the door open.

Two young officers stood on Laura's steps but neither made eye contact when she opened the door. Laura swallowed the unease that filled her and smiled at the men in front of her. They were probably just collecting for a charity or an event of some sort. Not that people ever showed up on their doorstep to solicit funds—that was all handled through a family foundation—but what other reason could there be?

"Can I help you, officers?"

"Ma'am." The older of the two—though not by much—took off his hat as he addressed her. "Are you Mrs. Laura Kensington?" he asked, as though that were necessary. Laura's face was well known. Years of appearing beside her famous husband and his iconic family in the media had seen to that.

Tiny fingers of fear ribboned Laura's spine. "Yes, that's me. How can I help you?"

"Would you mind if we came in and sat down, ma'am?" he asked and Laura glanced at the badges displayed on each man's uniform. He paused until Laura nodded and stepped back, opening the door wider to allow them to step through. They followed her to the sitting room and sat on the couch at her gesture.

"Can I offer you something to drink?" she asked, not at all sure she wanted to hear why they were here. She had given the housekeeper the afternoon off to ensure she had privacy for her phone call. Now, it seemed odd not to have someone hovering over her to take care of all of the niceties and polite offerings.

"No thank you, Mrs. Kensington. We're here about your husband, ma'am," said the older officer. The younger officer had yet to speak and still carefully avoided her eyes. Laura wished the older one would stop calling her ma'am. She was only twenty-five, and the title seemed more appropriate for her mother-in-law.

My husband?" Laura echoed, turning it into a question. Her mind whirled. *Why would the police be here about Patrick? What could the police possibly want with Patrick?* The tiny voice in the back of her mind told her she didn't want the answers.

"I'm afraid your husband has suffered a heart attack,

ma'am," the officer said. "His business partner found him in his office about an hour ago and tried to revive him."

Laura's hands shook so hard she had to fold them in her lap and grip one over the other to hold them still. Years of holding a well-honed mask in place were all that kept the façade in place.

"Tried to revive..." Her voice trailed off as the implication of what the man had said began to seep through her confusion. They weren't here because Patrick had done something illegal. They weren't here to ask about her husband's actions or search the house or question her.

"I'm sorry, Mrs. Kensington, but your husband didn't make it."

The breath whooshed out of Laura's body in one swift motion, but no new breath seemed to want to fill her lungs. The shaking in her hands only increased and she felt lightheaded.

She sucked in a breath and tried to steady herself. "Patrick?" She couldn't finish the thought. *Patrick is dead.* The tears that welled in her eyes weren't tears of anguish or sorrow, or anything else that a wife should feel for her husband.

They were tears of sheer and utter relief. After three years of terror, of never knowing what would happen to her, of walking on eggshells—after a month of planning her escape from the monster she'd married—he was gone. Laura tried to choke back a sob but it came out in a rough moan, wracking her body as relief and shock tore through her.

It's over. Could it really be this simple?

Clearly, the officers assumed she was upset by the news of her husband's death, and offered to call someone to come be with her. Laura couldn't blame them. That would be the natural assumption when telling someone their spouse had died.

"No." She shook her head. "I'd like to see my husband's body." If the men thought it was an odd request, they didn't show it.

"Ma'am," the officer repeated, "is there someone you'd like us to call before we take you over to the hospital? Another family member, maybe?"

Laura stood shakily from the couch. "No. I just need to get my purse," she said. She needed to go to the morgue. She needed to see him for herself. To know. To know, in her heart, he really was dead. That his hands would be stilled forever. That his lips wouldn't speak another cruel word. She needed to know she'd never look into his cold hard eyes again—eyes that had deceived the world…. Eyes that had deceived her at one time.

She needed proof that her nightmare was truly over.

CHAPTER TWO

D r. Josh Samuels signed out for the evening and waved to the two remaining nurses at the desk before getting on the elevator. He really needed to give more serious thought to retiring. Long shifts in the emergency room were designed for doctors a lot younger than he, even if he had cut back his hours fairly drastically in the last year. At the moment, he wanted nothing more than to kick off his shoes, open a bottle of wine, and read a good book.

But, thoughts of an evening of relaxation left his head the minute the elevator doors opened and he caught sight of Laura Kensington, flanked by two police officers in the lobby of the hospital. He'd treated Laura three months ago for a broken wrist and several months before that for cracked ribs and another month before that for concussion. He suspected more often than not, she didn't come to the emergency room when she was injured.

Josh saw abused women all the time in the ER and still felt compelled to help despite the odds. Getting the average woman to admit there was a problem and leave an abusive relationship was a challenge. Convincing one of America's most well-known wives, a woman who was practically royalty as the wife of one of *the* Kensingtons... Well, that had proved impossible. But, Josh wasn't about to give up. He'd been working on building a rapport with Laura and had reached out to her a few times. She'd been tolerant—she was too polite not to be—but she wouldn't admit there was anything going on. Perhaps the police officers with her this time meant she was ready to make a change, ready to seek help and get away from her husband.

"Laura?" Josh asked as he approached, forgetting the fact that he was no longer on shift. Laura looked pale and stunned as she turned toward him, but he couldn't see any outside evidence of injury on her body.

"Dr. Samuels," she said politely, ever playing the part of the wife of the powerful Patrick Kensington. He'd told her before to call him Josh but she never did.

"What's going on, Laura? Are you all right?" Josh looked from her to the officers, hoping for some kind of reading on the situation.

Laura seemed to be frozen as she answered and Josh quickly understood why. "Patrick is dead," she said as though she were delivering a report of what she planned to serve for dinner that night rather than a life-changing event. "Patrick had a heart attack."

"Oh, Laura," he said, not taking hold of her hands, but wanting to. "I'm so sorry."

But, no. He really wasn't sorry. He watched her face carefully to decipher how she was taking Patrick's death. He had yet to figure out if Laura had truly loved her husband, as many women who were abused did. Would she mourn his death and let the abuse fall to the back of her mind as she remembered the good in him? Or was this a relief to her? He'd always hoped he could convince her to walk away, and he had seen promise once or twice, but he also knew walking away would be a herculean effort for her. It was no simple thing for any woman in her situation, much less one who had the eyes of the world on her.

"I can take her down to the morgue, gentlemen," Josh said to the officers, who looked to Mrs. Kensington for confirmation. "I'm her doctor," he said.

It wasn't entirely true since he'd only ever treated her in the ER and she certainly wasn't currently under his care, but Josh wasn't worried about technicalities right now. He wanted to be sure Laura was all right.

She seemed numb as she nodded to the officers, who wasted no time tipping their caps to her and making a break for the door. They clearly hadn't relished the idea of taking her to the morgue to view her husband's body. Josh was more than happy to. He was fairly sure that the abuse she'd suffered over the years had been no small matter. If he could make a bit of difference for her, help her come to grips with what had happened and move on, he wanted to do it. And the first step would be helping her view the body of the man Josh was sure had tormented her.

LAURA STARED at the body in front of her and imagined Patrick's death was all a dream or a sick joke. The suddenness of her freedom left her reeling. She wasn't quite sure she wanted to trust it, to let herself believe it yet. She imagined he could still reach out to grab her. That he would sit up and trap her. That his hands would close around her throat once again, as he laughed at her struggle to draw breath.

She suppressed a shiver.

"Are you all right, Laura?" came Dr. Samuel's quiet voice. When she had first seen him in the lobby, she hadn't known what to think. The doctor had been trying to convince her to leave Patrick for a long time. Though she'd never told him what Patrick was doing, he always seemed to know. At first, his knowing eyes frightened her. If he pushed, if he insisted she get help, it would only make things worse. Thankfully, Patrick believed her when she'd said the doctor was trying to recruit her to serve on the hospital's charitable foundation board.

Over time, some of the doctor's advice broke through, and she understood he was right. She realized she needed to find the strength and courage to go. If she didn't leave soon, Patrick would kill her. And if he did, he'd be killing her unborn child with her. Laura couldn't put her baby at risk. She had put her plan of escape in motion as soon as she realized her baby would never be safe if she didn't leave her husband.

She looked up into the doctor's kind face. Hair like snow, gentle blue eyes. A questioning smile hovered on his lips. Something about him was always calming. Before she could think to say anything, his eyes darted to her arms and her stomach sank. She'd left the house in short sleeves and didn't realize she had been rubbing her hands up and down her upper arms, probably moving the sleeves up with each brush of her hands. She was normally careful to keep her sleeves in place.

Laura abruptly dropped her hands to her sides and glanced away. She swallowed the fear that clutched at her, grabbed hold, and didn't seem to want to let go. No one was supposed to learn her secrets. Not ever.

"I'm fine. Yes. Thank you, though. For asking, I mean.

But, I'm all right." Words seemed to blurt out from her lips now, as she tried to cover the awkward silence.

She looked back to her husband's body. She really *was* all right now. Patrick was gone. He couldn't hurt her anymore. He couldn't hurt her baby. One thought rang over and over in her head. *It's over. It's really over.*

"You look pale. Would you like some water or to take a seat?" he asked.

Laura shook her head. The smile she gave him was one born of practice.

"That's very nice of you, really, but I'm fine. Thank you." She'd pasted that smile on her face permanently, but both the smile and her words seemed at odds with the fact that she was viewing her dead husband's body.

The uncomfortable silence that settled between the two near-strangers was filled all too quickly by the sound of the automatic doors opening. Martha Kensington, Patrick's mother, and his notorious younger brother, Justin Kensington, were shown into the room by a technician, with Patrick's business partner, Alec Hall, at the rear. Martha and Alec were stone-faced, but Justin looked genuinely distressed.

Laura's step toward the doctor was instinctive, as was the way she cradled her stomach in an unmistakably protective gesture. Neither move went unnoticed. Martha's eyes narrowed on Laura a split second before the doctor stepped in front of her. Laura wasn't sure why this doctor had taken up her cause, why he was so willing to help her, but in that moment as she realized she wasn't free of the Kensingtons yet, she was grateful he was there by her side.

"Good morning. I'm Dr. Samuels." He extended his hand and merely waited, as if expecting the newcomers to introduce themselves, to explain their relationship to her husband. As if he didn't recognize them from the papers and television.

Justin met the doctor's eyes and shook his hand. Martha did not. Justin introduced everyone, then said, "I'd like my brother's body released as quickly as possible to this funeral home." Justin handed a card to Dr. Samuels. He, in turn, passed it to the morgue technician who had shown them in and now hovered awkwardly nearby.

Laura thought Martha would want to see her son, that she might show some sign of grief over losing him. But, no. Martha simply turned her back on Patrick's body and spoke in a cold, commanding voice, to no one in particular.

"We'll be taking my daughter-in-law home now, where she belongs. Laura, come."

Laura gasped. Martha's words were low—a warning and a command—one that was completely clear. Martha Kensington had no intention of letting Laura walk away with Patrick's baby. Tension coursed through the room feeling thick and weighty as realization hit. She wasn't free. Patrick's death had freed her from her husband's torment, but the Kensingtons would never let her go.

How stupid could I be? Laura knew in that moment that coming to the hospital had been a mistake. When she got the news, she should have left right away. No one would have thought anything of it if she told the police she wanted to be alone, that she'd go to the morgue when she was composed. If she'd done that, Laura could have taken the money she'd put away and the ID she'd hidden and left town before Martha Kensington could have stopped her.

She raised her chin and took a deep breath. There was no way in the world she was walking out of here with the Kensingtons. Freedom was in sight and she would grab it with both hands and hang on tight.

Dr. Samuels raised his hand, palm facing out, an appeasing gesture meant to diffuse, but a firm one nonetheless. "I'm sorry, Mrs. Kensington. I can't allow that."

Martha looked stunned at the refusal. She drew her already tall form up to its full height. "She'll come home with us. She's pregnant, doctor. She needs to be with family so we can care for the baby. *We're* the baby's family."

Laura opened her mouth to speak, although she wasn't sure what she intended to say. But, the doctor was there for her once again, intervening with Martha in a way Laura wasn't sure she could have. Her relationship with her mother-in-law was not a loving one. In fact, in many ways, Martha frightened her more than Patrick had and whatever lifeline Dr. Samuel was throwing her, she would take.

"Then I'm sure you understand, for the safety of the baby, I cannot let Laura go with you. She's suffered quite an emotional blow this evening."

"Nonsense. We have a private physician who can meet us at the house," Martha said. Justin shifted next to her looking from Laura to his mother and back again, seemingly undecided as to whether to support his mother or listen to the doctor. Alec stepped forward as if to join the debate, but the doctor raised a hand again.

"Now, I'm sure you'll agree, we all want the best for Laura *and* the baby. By the time you get her home, she could be in a state of shock, putting both Laura and the baby at risk," Dr. Samuels said. "I'm going to keep her here under observation. We'll monitor the baby for twenty-four to forty-eight hours and be sure there are no complications or ill-effects from the shock."

CHAPTER THREE

Laura was stunned. No one challenged the Kensington family. Not only had Dr. Samuels challenged them, it appeared to have worked. The Kensingtons had no response for Dr. Samuels as he waltzed her out of the room. She suddenly felt five years old as opposed to her twenty-five years, and she felt the need to cling to the doctor's hand like a little girl would cling to her mother's.

"I don't..." Laura didn't know what to say as they waited for the elevator.

"Don't say anything. Wait 'til we're on the elevator. Don't turn around and look at them. Just look straight ahead and walk away as if nothing is wrong," the doctor said quietly.

Laura was silent as they rode two flights up. When the doors slid open, the older gentleman led her off the elevator to a small office. He shut the door and helped her to a couch, then sat across from her. At that point, Laura would be lying if she said she wasn't shaking. She honestly had no idea what to make of what had just happened, but she was feeling more than overwhelmed by the events of the last hour. She needed to get it together. She needed a plan.

The doctor leaned forward and she felt compelled to look into his kind eyes. He didn't know it, but he had been a big part of her decision to leave Patrick. Well, not the decision itself so much—that had been more to do with her pregnancy than anything the doctor had said—but he had planted the seeds of courage to start thinking about leaving even before she knew about the baby. Laura's head spun as the doctor looked at her, and waited patiently.

Her husband was dead. For two minutes while she'd looked at his body, she'd felt relief. She'd thought she was finally free. But she wasn't, and it was foolish to think freedom would ever come easily for her. Patrick's mother would now be even more committed to keeping Laura and the baby in the fold because her son was gone. Martha would want to keep close any part of Patrick that she could still control—Laura and her baby.

No, that wasn't exactly right. Once the baby was born, Martha would have no need for Laura. She knew in her heart Martha would try to take her baby. She'd fight for custody and she'd fight dirty. Martha Kensington didn't know any other way to be. The fear that she had lived with for three years of marriage began to churn deep in her stomach, rising up her throat to steal the breath from her body.

The doctor's gentle voice broke into Laura's thoughts. "Laura, do you need to get away from your husband's family?" he asked cautiously as though he didn't want to offend her with the assumption.

Laura heard a small sob and realized it had come from her. She nodded. "Yes. I think I do." *How could this be happening? Could Martha really take my baby?* Maybe Laura was just overreacting from the shock of seeing

Patrick's body. She must be. This couldn't really be happening.

"No. No, I'm sure I... I don't know," she said. The Kensingtons were now down to Martha and Justin. Laura hadn't seen enough of Justin to know what he would do. He had always traveled and hardly saw the family any longer. But, in truth, it was Martha she feared. Could Martha use her wealth and influence to take her child from her? Now that Patrick was dead, couldn't Laura stand and fight instead of running? Shouldn't she be able to take on Martha and win?

"I had plans to leave next week." She swallowed and closed her eyes as tears dropped, but continued. It was suddenly important to her that this doctor know she'd had the guts to walk away from Patrick before he'd died. At least, she *thought* she would have had the guts to go through with her plan.

"I sold jewelry Patrick wouldn't know was missing, jewelry that normally sits in our safety deposit box between events. I bought a new identity and was ready to run next week." Laura wrapped her arms around her belly, hugging herself tightly.

"I think that's wonderful, Laura. I knew you had it in you to leave someday."

But Laura had a feeling he had been ready to give up hope on her. He'd been trying for close to a year and she had never admitted the abuse, much less given him hope she would leave.

"Do you have family you can go to? Anyone who can take you in? Help you if the Kensingtons try to fight for custody?"

Laura's head snapped up. How had he read the situation so clearly?

Would Martha do that? Fight for custody?

"Laura, do you have family you can call?" he tried again.

No. There's no one left. Laura tried not to think about her brother. It hurt too much to know he was dead. Her mother had died long before Laura was old enough to remember, but her brother had always been the one bright spot in her life. When his life was taken in a car accident only a few months after her marriage to Patrick, she'd lost the last of the family she cared about.

Laura shook her head. "No. No family."

Her thoughts shifted back to Martha and the odd statements she'd made about the baby being *her* family, being a Kensington. "I'm probably overreacting," she whispered softly, but there was little conviction to the statement.

As she pictured what Martha Kensington might be capable of when it came to getting her grandchild, fear latched onto her, hard and deep and bone chilling. The Kensington family wielded power within this state like no other and she had wealth to back it up. Laura would have money from Patrick's estate, but there was no telling if that would be enough. No. She wouldn't risk it. *Couldn't* risk it. Not when it came to her unborn child.

The doctor's voice cut through her thoughts once more. "Can you get to the money you saved?"

"I buried it in a pot in my greenhouse. It's the one place he never goes. *Went.* The one place he never went."

"I think we've bought a little time by telling your mother-in-law I'd check you into the hospital. I can drive you to your home to get the money and then we can get you out of here. You can get a good head start on the Kensingtons before they realize you're gone."

Laura shook her head at the man sitting across from her. "I don't understand. Why are you helping me?" Her voice shook, but she took a deep breath, then swallowed hard. She would get herself under control. She would handle this.

The doctor seemed to fortify himself with his own deep breath before he answered. "When I saw you that first time in my ER, you reminded me so much of my own daughter. She's just about your age. I couldn't imagine what it would be like to know my daughter was being hurt like I knew you were." Laura flinched but he continued, "I just want to help you start again. Whatever it was that brought you to this spot, that brought you to this marriage, you deserve some help in getting out of it." His smile was tender.

Tears burned at Laura's eyes. Fear, humiliation, and confusion vied for top position in her mind. She stood and paced at the far end of the office, for some reason feeling the need to reiterate her plan to leave, to explain that she wasn't just a victim. She was more than that. Not at first, she hadn't been, but now she was stronger. She'd been getting stronger and stronger by the day.

"When I got pregnant, I knew I had to leave. I knew I couldn't risk staying there with the baby. Not with the way..." She couldn't finish that sentence. She couldn't tell anyone what her husband had been doing to her, even though it was clear the doctor knew some of it.

Laura took a deep breath and made a decision. She needed to trust this doctor. He'd been trying to offer her a lifeline for months now, and it was time she took it. "Yes. I think I need to get the money and leave. I don't want Martha Kensington anywhere near my baby. She raised one monster. I'm not going to let her have anything to do with raising my child. I don't have much money put aside, but I have enough for a security deposit and a few months' rent while I find work." Laura didn't bother to tell the doctor that the only thing she could get a job doing was waitressing or maybe working as a hostess in a restaurant. She had no degree, no experience other than waitressing and it was old experience, at that.

Dr. Samuels stood and gathered his coat and keys then handed Laura her purse. As they left the hospital, she thought for a minute that she should probably just call a taxi to take her home for her things and then go to the airport, but when he told her where he would pick her up at the outer edge of the parking lot, she found herself leaving with him instead. The truth was, she didn't want to do this alone right now and there wasn't anyone else for her to turn to. Laura swallowed her doubts and grabbed hold of her conviction. She was leaving. She was finished being a Kensington. She was finished letting Martha have any hold over her. For better or worse, it was time to run.

CHAPTER FOUR

When they turned onto the street where she and Patrick lived, Laura was stunned. The front of the house was crawling with reporters. They spilled out onto the sidewalk, as enormous antennae towered over news vans and pierced the sky. The news of Patrick's death had gotten out.

"Change of plans," the doctor muttered as he turned down a side street a block before they reached the house.

Laura turned and looked out the back window of the car and took a deep breath. She needed a new plan. She thought of the money, her ID. Her mind also flashed to that USB drive taped to the bottom of a drawer in her kitchen. She hadn't planned to touch it when she ran, but now that Patrick was dead... Maybe she should take it with her as well. If she could just get into the house. She glanced at her phone to check the time and thought to herself that she'd need to get rid of her phone if she wanted to hide.

She spoke more to herself than to the doctor at this point as she searched in her purse for her wallet. "The bank is closed, but if you can take me to an ATM, I'll take out what I can and then figure out where to go from here. I think there's a limit on what I can take from the ATM in one day. Five hundred dollars, maybe?"

"I can take another five hundred dollars out of my account for you, so you'll have a little more. You won't be able to get a new identity right away, but we can get you to a safe place. Airlines are subject to very strict regulations nowadays so your husband's family shouldn't be able to find out what plane you took. By the time they realize you're missing, you'll be long gone."

"I can't take your money," Laura said, shaking her head. "Besides, it isn't enough for rent and the deposit on any apartment. I can take money from my ATM and find a hotel to stay in nearby until I can get to the money in the greenhouse or the bank on Monday."

The doctor raised an eyebrow. "Do you really think that's a good idea?"

"No," Laura admitted, "but I don't see any other option."

She felt weak and sick to her stomach at the thought of not leaving the area right away. She honestly didn't know if she was being rational or not, but everything in her was screaming to put distance between herself and the Kensingtons right now. And, once again, she remembered the look of fear in Patrick's eyes when he'd hidden the USB drive. A tickle of doubt scratched at the edge of her brain as she shoved the memory aside.

She fought back another wave of tears. She would not cry again. No amount of tears would help the situation.

"Do you have any friends you can stay with?"

She shook her head. The friends she'd had in New Jersey before she married Patrick stopped calling when she made excuses not to talk to them or see them. The shame of having to lie to them about her marriage had made her tuck herself away from anyone who would question too much or see through her act. Of course, they'd all assumed she thought she was too good for them after marrying into the Kensington clan. *Ha!* The joke had been on her, hadn't it?

And the friends she had in Connecticut—well, they weren't truly friends. Just country club acquaintances. None of them would take her in and hide her from Martha Kensington.

They were quiet for a minute before the doctor cracked a wide smile. "I know a place you can go while you get on your feet."

Laura cringed. She had a feeling she knew what he was going to say, and the idea of going to a shelter, of answering questions and letting anyone else know what was going on made her stomach clench even more.

"I've got a friend who owns a ranch in Texas. I spend a few weeks there every summer. It's the perfect place for you to figure things out, to clear your head and start again, and I just know May would love to have you." He drew a cell phone out of his pocket and keyed through the contacts before selecting one.

"How do you feel about Texas?" he asked her, holding the phone in his hand without hitting send as though asking her whether to make the call or not.

Texas? She couldn't possibly show up on the doorstep of a stranger, even if Dr. Samuels said it was all right. There was nothing all right about doing something like that.

Laura smiled, but it felt weak. If she didn't go where he suggested, where would she go? Even if she took Dr. Samuel's five hundred dollars along with hers, she couldn't use her ATM or credit cards again unless she wanted to be tracked after she left. She wasn't exactly swimming in options. Every penny in cash she had was buried in a flower pot, and she'd have to cross a line of reporters to get to it. Reporters who would no doubt print pictures of her arriving home, blowing the lead she had. If the Kensingtons saw that she wasn't in the hospital, they'd be on her that much faster.

"I promise," he said. "May would really love the company."

Laura looked back over her shoulder toward the house. Even if she could push through the news reporters, the thought of going back into the house she'd shared with Patrick... She just couldn't do that. She couldn't go back now.

"Texas it is," she said more to herself than to the doctor who was now speaking with someone on the other end of the phone.

"May? It's Josh. I need a favor." The doctor listened for a moment before speaking again. "I'm sending someone to you. I need you to keep her safe with you at the ranch."

There was another pause as he listened, and then turned to Laura and nodded with a big grin. "I'll see if I can get her on a flight right away and then she'll take the bus from Austin. I'm not sure exactly what day she'll arrive," he said, glancing at Laura.

The doctor listened again. "Thank you. Oh, and May? Don't contact me for a while. I'll get in touch in a few weeks. I don't want any contact between us that might let someone track her right now, so let's keep it to this one call."

Laura looked over at the man who was helping her flee. She dug deep and found the strength she'd built up while living with Patrick over the past three years. She would *not* let his family take the baby, and she'd be damned if she'd let them have any part in raising her child. The woman who had raised her monster of a husband wouldn't be coming anywhere near her baby.

She'd go to Texas long enough to get her bearings and come up with a plan. She'd spend a few days there to figure out her next move. Then she'd move on, as planned, and find a job somewhere. She'd only stay in one place a few weeks at a time if she could manage it, until she was certain the Kensingtons had given up their search for her.

Laura took a deep breath and nodded at the doctor. *Texas.*

CHAPTER FIVE

C ade Bishop loved it when hours of patience paid off and he made a connection with a frightened animal. The telltale sign might be a low whinny from a horse or being allowed to check out the new kittens of a feral cat. Most often, it happened in subtle ways, with little changes in the animal happening here or there over time. But Red had offered her trust suddenly and completely this morning. For the rust-colored mixed-breed dog he'd found hurt and wandering on the highway four weeks ago, her trust came as a floodgate opening rather than a trickle.

For weeks, Cade sat calmly and quietly near Red's food bowl during mealtimes. He never moved or attempted to approach her while she ate. There were no strings attached. No pushing. He simply sat and let her get used to his smell, to the sight of him, to slight movements. Sometimes he talked — nonsensical ramblings about his day. Sometimes he didn't. At times, she spooked and ran away. When that happened, Cade just waited. He knew she'd come back on her own, in her own time.

Today, after eating, Red stood staring at Cade for a long

time. She appeared calm, but those deep round-platter eyes of hers still seemed to take in everything. She looked as if she were weighing, balancing something in her mind. Maybe some risk versus some reward? Cade often wished he could read the minds of the animals he worked with.

As he watched her, she splayed her front legs ever so slightly and dipped her head. It wasn't truly a play bow. It was the ghost of a playful bow, but enough of an invitation that Cade caught it.

He turned toward her and mirrored her gesture, arms outward and head dipped. He might not be a dog, but apparently his mimicry was good enough for Red. Her response was instantaneous. She flew into his arms, nearly knocking him on his butt. Twenty minutes later, she was still in Cade's arms. She spun over and over, snuggling and whirling in the circle his arms created, as if she needed human contact more than she needed air.

Cade laughed as she circled, in awe of the need she had for this connection and the way she let herself trust him after so much time. There really wasn't anything on earth that compared to seeing a hurt or injured animal find love and trust again. Though the ice was now broken, he knew Red would need to learn to trust other people too. She needed to figure out that most humans were okay, even though he would lay money on the fact that at some point humans had hurt her.

As Red settled down at the end of her spontaneous snuggle-fest, he stood slowly, talking to her quietly as he rose. "Come on, girl. Let's take a walk out to the paddock and see Millie."

She took a few cautious steps back as Cade rose to his full height, as if she still weren't completely sure, but quickly returned to his side and followed him out through the large open doors at the end of the barn. Together, they walked out to visit Millie, an old quarter horse he was nursing back to health.

Millie and Red weren't the usual kind of animals Cade worked with. Most of his time on the ranch was devoted to working with retired horses from various racetracks around Texas. Cade helped the horses adjust to life off the track and found new career paths for them. Some went to homes as pets, while others went into dressage or eventing, or began second careers as hunter jumpers. But Cade was drawn to animals who had been neglected or abused and never could resist helping animals like Millie and Red.

He suspected Red had been abused, but didn't know for sure. She had been half starved and frightened out of her wits when he found her. It was possible she was only under socialized, but the way she shied away from any person she came in contact with, coupled with the scars that trimmed her body, made him think it had been more than simply not being socialized properly.

In Millie's case, he knew exactly what had happened. She had been neglected. She'd been seized from an owner who left her in a stall that likely hadn't seen a pitchfork or fresh hay in a month. She was skin and bones when she came to the ranch, and she had horrible thrush in her hooves from standing in her own waste and filth. County animal control had seized Millie and asked Cade for help, which he'd gladly given. After winning the court case against the owner, the county signed ownership over to Cade. He would rehab her and then find her the right home when the time came.

"She looks better and better, don't you think?" Cade asked Red, who perked her ears up and looked up at him, an assessing gleam in her eyes.

Millie came to the fence and nickered. Miraculously, her trust in humans had never dwindled. She only needed time to fatten up and let her hooves heal. She was getting the dry bedding she needed, quality hay, and treatment for her hooves now that she was with Cade. When she was in better shape, Cade would ride her to see if, as he suspected, she'd make a nice horse for a child or a riding school. When he'd put a saddle on her a few days ago, she accepted it calmly and patiently. That patience could be a blessing to a child learning to ride.

"Hey, girl." Cade rubbed the white blaze between Millie's eyes as she stretched out her neck and turned her head to push against his hand. When he dropped his hand, she shoved her head against his shoulder. Millie was no dummy—she knew Cade kept mints in his chest pocket, and she never let him leave without getting at least one.

"Yes, ma'am." Cade laughed. He pulled out a mint and fed it to the mare on the flat of his hand.

"Hoo, boy. Is that Red?" Cade's brother Shane spoke from a healthy ten feet away, but even so, Red's head ducked and she skittered behind Cade.

Cade looked at his brother who hung back, as always. Shane didn't work the animals on the ranch like Cade, and he didn't have the natural ability Cade had with them, but he had learned to give them space until Cade told him he could come closer. A couple of horses nipping at him and the consequent holes in his suit coats and dress shirts had taught him that, over the years.

"Yup. She had a bit of a breakthrough this morning— apparently she needed snuggling more than she needed her safety zone," Cade said. "What're you doing here on a weekday? Not that we don't love seeing your ugly face, but to what do we owe the honor?"

Shane didn't live and work on the ranch the way Cade did. He spent the week in town at his law firm doing everything from creating wills to representing people in court. He usually only came out to the ranch on weekends.

It always made Cade itch when he saw Shane wearing a suit. Although he and Shane could be twins with their dark hair and emerald-green eyes and their six-two matching heights, Cade wouldn't be caught dead in a suit. And sometimes, he was convinced Shane wouldn't be caught dead without one. Cade's dusty Stetson identified him as much as the neatly knotted tie identified Shane.

"Just had to bring some papers out for Mama to sign. She's setting up another scholarship fund," Shane answered, still watching Red in amazement as she stood calmly behind Cade's legs.

"I'll walk you up to the house," Cade said. "I'm starving." The brothers turned and walked up toward the main house while Red trailed behind at a safe distance.

"Who's the new fund for?" he asked as they walked.

Their mother, May Bishop, created scholarships by design whenever someone needed something that she was in a position to help with. After the initial person received their scholarship through the fund, she would keep it going, looking for others who needed help, year after year. She had funds for farmers who had suffered a poor crop due to natural causes, a fund for single mothers to pay for car or home repairs, and a number of funds for students pursuing different degrees.

"Amanda Ayers. She was short a few thousand dollars for nursing school. She has almost enough credits to graduate. Mama is making sure she can afford it."

Cade nodded.

"I saw Lacey in town the other day. She looks better," Shane said.

Cade didn't answer right away. It had been a year since he and Lacey had broken up, and he still wasn't too keen to talk about her. Shane should have known that.

"Yeah? She visiting her mom?" he finally asked, as they neared the front porch.

Shane nodded and slipped his suit coat off, folding it over his arm. "She's still living in Austin with her dad. She's starting school there in the fall. Plans to study fashion design or something."

"Good. That's good for her," Cade said and nodded. He meant it. He wished Lacey well. At one time, he thought they would spend the rest of their lives together, but things began to unravel the last year they were together, and he had known they weren't meant for each other.

The two men wiped off their feet before walking into the ranch's welcoming kitchen.

May Bishop stood at the counter, talking into her cell phone. "Okay, Josh. We'll see her when she gets here," she said and then disconnected the phone and tucked it into her apron pocket.

"Hi, Mama," Shane said, bending to kiss the small woman.

"Sit, boys," May said. She put a basket of bread on the table.

Cade noticed the first hints of gray in her long dark braids, and how heavily she rested the right side of her body on her cane. The car accident that had taken their father's life had left their mother with serious injuries, but she didn't often let them slow her down.

May loved nothing more than to have her boys at the table where she could feed them. To her, food was love.

There was no talk as the men ate, but that was typical. The Bishop Boys, as they were referred to in town, were well known for their appetites. When there was food in front of them, they ate with undivided focus. They tended to eat enormous quantities, particularly when their mother cooked meals like this. Thankfully, they were active enough to keep the food from thickening their waistlines. Cade with his work on the ranch, and Shane, running miles each day while thinking through cases and client problems.

When there wasn't a scrap of food left, conversation began.

"What did Uncle Josh have to say?" Cade asked.

Josh Samuels wasn't really Shane and Cade's uncle. He had grown up with May and her late husband, Jim Bishop, and Shane and Cade considered him family. He was a physician now, and May had leaned on him when her husband died ten years ago. It wasn't uncommon for him to spend a couple of weeks at the ranch in the summer.

"It was an odd call, actually. He's sending someone out here to stay with us. He asked us not to contact him about her, but to keep her safe when she gets here. Says he isn't sure exactly when she'll arrive."

Shane rubbed his brow, frowning, and Cade knew what was coming. Shane was a worrier. He worried about anything and everything, even when there wasn't a damn thing to worry about.

"Mama, that sounds a little...off. Did he tell you anything else about who she is or why she's coming? Why wouldn't he know when we should expect her?" Shane asked as he and Cade ferried dirty dishes to the sink. Cade kept quiet. He didn't see anything wrong with someone coming to the ranch if they needed help, and he knew their mother would see it that way, too. And even if he didn't agree with her, arguing with their mother once she set her mind on something was useless.

"I don't know," May said mildly, "but I'm sure we'll find out when our guest gets here."

Shane let it rest for a few minutes while they washed plates, but Cade could tell he wasn't going to let it drop.

"Did he say anything else about her? Does he know her well? And what does 'keep her safe' mean?" Shane asked. He rinsed the soap off a dish under the faucet and handed it to Cade to dry. "It sounds like this woman could be bringing a world of trouble with her."

May let some of her annoyance show. "I don't know, Shane, and I don't need to know. Josh asked for our help and we're going to give it to him. It's as simple as that."

"Mama," Shane's tone said he disagreed. "People try to take advantage of older people all the time. It's well known you have money. What if she's some kind of scam artist?"

Cade took a big sidestep away from his brother. Shane didn't know when to back down when facing off against their mother. He hadn't figured out it was useless to argue with her. And, he sure hadn't figured out that talking about someone taking advantage of the elderly was a surefire way to tick her off.

"Don't you 'Mama' me. After all that man has done for us, I'm not about to ask questions when he needs help, and neither should either of you. We can take in animals left and right, but you want to shut your doors to a human being? A human being your Uncle Josh sent our way to look after? Shame on you. And, I'm not some old fool who can be conned or scammed. What do you think she did? Found out Josh knows me and somehow figured out a way to get him to send her here? That's just silly. Not to mention what that says about your confidence in me. Do you think I'm just going to hand her my checkbook when she walks through the door?"

Cade stifled a laugh. Truth was, Mama *would* hand the woman her checkbook if she thought she needed money badly enough.

Cade took another step away from Shane and swallowed a grin, as May gave them both one of her I've-spoken-and-the-subject-is-closed looks. "I expect she'll be here in the next few days. We'll find out all we need to know about the situation then."

Shane raised his eyebrows at Cade but didn't say a word. Guess it was time to get ready for company.

CHAPTER SIX

L aura shifted in the navy blue seat of the greyhound bus. It had taken far too many hours of sitting still to get to the hill country of Texas. There hadn't been a flight to Austin for eight hours, and even though Josh volunteered to sit with her in the airport, she had needed to do this on her own. She wanted to find the inner strength to leave without leaning on Josh any more than she already had.

But she'd still felt as though every person who passed her as she waited in the airport was sent by the Kensingtons —to take her back. She held her breath countless times when a stranger seemed to look at her with knowing eyes, and had nearly run in a panic when one man walked right up to her and asked the time.

Josh dropped her at the airport, and she'd had to pass through security alone. At the time, Laura felt an irrational panic, as if she'd cut her final lifeline, her tether to safety. Once she finally boarded the plane, she'd been sick to her stomach for most of the flight, and now the never-ending bus ride between the airport and the ranch wasn't making her feel any better. What had started out as a comfortable seat, now felt like a torture device designed to tie her back in knots and put her legs to sleep.

She had been cursed with an overly sensitive nose since the early weeks of her pregnancy, and that made the ride difficult to deal with. So many people in a confined space led to a mixture of odors that was unpleasant, at best. She nibbled crackers and got off the bus at each stop for a few gulps of air that was fresher than on board. She felt as if she would need to walk and move and stretch for days before she'd be ready to sit down again.

The discomfort took her mind off the fact that she didn't know the people she was headed to see and had no idea what to expect. Dr. Samuels—no, *Josh*, he'd told her to call him Josh—had told her these people were like family; they'd take her in without question and she would be safe and welcomed there. That didn't change the fact that Laura hated the idea of simply showing up on someone's doorstep and for another handout. Taking money from Josh had been hard enough. Letting complete strangers take her in would be even harder to swallow.

It had been whipped into Laura as a little girl that handouts were not to be accepted, regardless of the need—but she had to think of her unborn child. Right now, there were no other options. She couldn't keep her baby safe and escape the overwhelming power of the Kensington family if she'd remained in their sphere of influence. So here she was, about to be delivered to Texas Hill Country.

An hour later, Laura stepped off the bus carrying the small backpack Josh had bought for her. He had loaded it with a few pairs of pants and shirts from Walmart along with toiletries. She'd cleaned herself up in the Austin Airport, but after four hours on a bus, she felt wrinkled and mussed beyond repair.

Laura looked across the street as the bus pulled out with a small whirlwind of orange dust in its wake. It had let her off just where Josh said it would at Jansen's Feed Store. She swallowed the last bit of pride she had left, lifted her eyes, and crossed the road. This was for her child, and for her child, she could do anything. Even if it meant asking complete strangers for a handout.

A small bell announced her arrival in the feed store, and a few older gentlemen looked up from a table at the back of the room where they played cards. No one showed any sign that they recognized who she was, so her current rumpled condition must have hidden the fact that she was Laura Kensington—a woman most would recognize from news reports on the famous family. When her father-in-law was alive, his status as a United States senator and the family's lengthy history of public service had kept them front and center in tabloids as well as legitimate news sources.

The current generation, Laura's husband and his brother, Justin, had found the limelight for different reasons —because of their antics as playboys in their early twenties rather than through service. Both had shunned careers in politics. Patrick had started his real estate development business with his business partner, Alec, but Justin had dismissed the business world altogether. He had traveled the world at the expense of a trust fund large enough for him to continue on for decades in that manner, if he chose.

"Help you, miss?"

Laura turned to see a man on her right with a long gray beard. He wore a cap with a large fish on it and peered at her through wire-rimmed glasses.

"Yes, I'm looking for Tom Jansen. Can you please tell me where I might find him?" Laura asked. She hated this. Despised the idea of walking in off the street and asking for a ride the way Josh had told her to. He said they'd think nothing of it, but it didn't seem right to her.

She felt his eyes take her in from head to toe. It wasn't a leering look or inappropriate in any way. It was the way a local takes in someone who clearly isn't from the area. When his eyes made it back to her face, they were kind and warm.

"You got him. What can I do fer ya?"

"I...uh... Josh Samuels told me I might be able to find a ride out to the Bishop Ranch if I came in here." Laura looked toward the road where the bus had dropped her moments before. "I just came in by bus, and I don't have a way out to the ranch. I wasn't sure exactly when I'd arrive, so..." Laura pressed her lips shut, aware that she was babbling. Nothing was coming out as gracefully as she'd have liked.

The man in front of her appeared to think nothing of someone walking in off the street and asking for a ride. He simply smiled and turned to the group of men playing cards.

"Seth, you heading out toward May Bishop's place? Young lady here needs a ride," he called to one of the men.

A man who looked as though he'd spent the last forty years tanning his hide in the Texas sun threw down his cards and put a well-worn Stetson hat on his head. "You bet. Headed that way right now," he said. He smiled at her, but she sensed he would have stayed to play cards all day if she hadn't walked in and forced a change of his plans.

"Oh, I don't want to cause you any trouble. Are you sure you're ready to leave?" Laura asked, but the man was already talking a mile a minute about how he was headed that way and could he take her bag for her and "is this all you have? Just this little bag?" The situation was surreal, to say the least.

Laura gave a weak smile to Tom Jansen and followed Seth out to a beat-up truck parked in front of the feed store. The back was piled high with sacks of feed and a wooden crate filled with assorted tools, packages, and a small tray of plants.

Seth held the passenger door for her. Laura braced herself, knowing he'd touch an elbow or arm to help her into the truck. She knew from experience that the slightest touch would send a wave of nausea and fear through her, but if she anticipated it ahead of time and focused on it, she could cover any flinching. Laura gritted her teeth and held herself still while he helped her into the truck.

Seth walked around to the other side and settled himself next to her, then began a stream of chatter that didn't seem to require any response from her.

"Visiting May and her boys? *Hmmm*. You'll love it out at the ranch. First time you've been here, I'd guess. I would've seen ya if you'd been out here before. I make the trip to Jansen's twice a week, to keep up with what's going on. My wife, Joelle—you'll meet her soon if you stay for long —she can't get around much nowadays so she stays up at the house. I bring back all the news from town when I come out. She likes to hear what everyone's up to."

As Seth talked, Laura wondered how wise it was to come here. The way he spoke, it seemed as though everyone in a fifty-mile radius would know she was here within ten minutes. What on earth had she done, putting her trust in a stranger and taking his word that coming here to Texas, of all places, was the right thing to do?

She'd done what she had to do, that's what she'd done. She'd have to go to the Bishop Ranch and then decide if it was the right place to be. She still had nearly six hundred dollars after buying a one-way ticket from Connecticut to

Austin and paying her bus fare out to Evers, Texas. It wasn't nearly the amount she'd received when she sold her jewelry, but getting to that money was too risky for now.

Laura watched the road and tried to listen as Seth talked next to her, but she didn't process much of what he was saying. It seemed they were miles from nowhere, surrounded by fields dotted with cattle and barbed-wire fences. Seth slowed and turned at a wide wrought-iron gate anchored on either side by pillars of white stone. A looming sign over the entrance featured scrolled ironwork with large Iron Bs on either end with a horse in the center.

It struck Laura as odd that the stone pillars were connected to wire fencing around the rest of the land, but that looked like the way it was done out here—ornate entrances flanked by nothing but strands of wire.

"Well, this is it. I'll take you on up to the main house where May'll be. Cade's probably out in the barns working with those animals he's always taking in, and Shane'll be in town. I expect you'll want time to visit with May and get settled in before you see the rest of the family," Seth said as he drove down a long dirt road with trees on both sides and green fields beyond.

Laura nodded as he talked and didn't let on that she had no idea who Cade or Shane were and that Josh had only told her to ask for May. Laura was good at acting. She'd been acting for the last three years so it came pretty easy now. Seth probably assumed she knew all the Bishops well if she was coming for a visit, and she couldn't blame him for that.

A large red barn stood off to the left, looking a lot larger and brighter than she'd expected. When Laura thought of barns, she pictured faded rust-colored paint, run down in appearance, and sided with weather-beaten wood. This barn looked new and modern.

Seth must have read her mind. "They put that new barn in about two years ago. Nothing but state of the art for Cade's rescues," he said with a laugh, but Laura didn't know what he meant. She offered a small smile anyway.

They continued up the dirt road and she saw a paved walkway running alongside the road. She apparently had a lot to learn about ranches. She never would have imagined a paved walkway on a ranch.

As the house came into view—a large house made of the same white stone as the pillars out front—she noticed a large white wraparound porch. A small woman came out leaning heavily on a cane. On the porch sat a wheelchair, perhaps explaining the paved walkway. The woman waved, and a warm smile took over her open face.

For reasons she couldn't explain, Laura was relieved. At that moment, she felt as though everything might be all right after all. As though she hadn't just lived a nightmare, had her world upended, and gone on the run. Somehow, in this older woman's smile, Laura found a sliver of peace.

CHAPTER SEVEN

C ade watched Shane unfold himself from the sensible sedan he'd parked in front of the barn. Cade thought a man who was six-two should have a bigger car, but Shane just wanted a sensible, well-made, moderately-priced car. It seemed silly not to get something bigger he'd fit in comfortably, and that didn't make him look like a sardine crammed into a tin can.

Cade had called Shane as soon as he saw Seth drop off their mysterious visitor, but when his brother started in with questions about her, he regretted making the call.

"Did you see her? What did she look like?" Shane asked as he approached.

"Couldn't really see anything. Seth dropped her off up at the house and must have said 'hi' to Mama before he drove off. That was it," Cade said with a shrug.

"You didn't see anything else?" Shane asked, squinting against the glare of the sun. "Do you think she's a friend of Uncle Josh's daughter? Was she young? Old?"

Cade laughed and kept walking. "I think you can relax, Shane. She hardly looked like a crazed killer, and I doubt

Uncle Josh would send a con artist Mama's way. What's got you so worked up about this?"

"Heck, I don't know. I just worry about Mama nowadays. I know she likes setting up scholarship funds and helping everyone out, but I wish she'd do it anonymously. It's like sticking a huge billboard out on the road that says: 'I've got money, and you can take advantage of me if you want.' It makes her vulnerable to all kinds of people."

Cade shook his head at his brother as they took the porch steps two at a time together. "I think law school made you bitter and pessimistic, brother."

A scowl was the only answer he got before they were at the door, looking through the inset window at the woman who had arrived less than half an hour before.

Cade hadn't expected anyone like the petite blonde woman who sat at his mother's kitchen table, hands wrapped around a mug as if she needed its heat. He wasn't sure what he expected, but he knew she wasn't it. She had long white-blonde hair that fell over her shoulders in a silky wave. Her eyes were brown, but darkened in shadow as if she needed to sleep for several days to make up for deprivation or stress. There was something hauntingly familiar about her, but the image was too vague for him to figure it out.

As he watched through the window, her beauty was plain for any to see, but it was her body language that caught his attention. She looked ready to flee at any moment. Her eyes froze on him and Shane when she saw them through the glass. Sure enough, she stood and braced herself as soon as Cade turned the door handle to walk into the kitchen. What she was braced against, he didn't know.

Cade saw her tense, but also thought he saw a conscious

effort to relax her body seconds later, as if she had practiced shielding her internal state for some time now.

"Hey, Mama. We saw our guest had arrived and thought we'd come say hello." Cade removed his hat and nodded at the woman watching him with wary eyes.

"Boys, this is Laura. Laura, these are my boys. You'll see Cade here on the ranch every day. Shane lives in town and works in his office there, but you'll see him here every few days as well."

"It's a pleasure to meet you," came her quiet response. She was dignified, almost regal, as if she'd been trained how to hold herself, how to engage with people. How to put on the right show for those who watched.

Laura sat down again. Apparently, she had decided not to run but Cade couldn't help noticing the way she slid her backpack closer to her.

"How do you know our Uncle Josh?" Shane dug right into the questions as he always did, earning frowns from Mama and an eye roll from Cade.

"Will you excuse us a minute, Laura? Shane, in the den." May Bishop didn't request that her son join her, and she didn't wait for his response. It was an order. She walked into the adjoining room and Cade knew she expected Shane to follow. Cade went along, as well, sensing Laura wouldn't feel comfortable being left alone with him so soon after meeting him.

Cade shut the door behind them to keep the conversation from Laura's ears, but he imagined she would guess they were arguing anyway.

"Shane, I won't say this again. That woman is welcome in my home and you won't make her feel otherwise. Do you understand me?"

"Mama, you don't know anything about her. She looks

like trouble's chasing hot on her tail, and we need to know what kind of trouble that is."

May let out a huff of laughter but there was censure rather than humor in it. "You saw all that from one glance at that poor woman?"

Cade stared out the window at the long dusty drive that led to the house, waiting for his mother and brother to hash things out. He had only spent thirty seconds with the woman, same as Shane, but he could also see she was running scared. It seemed clear that the woman wouldn't be here if she didn't need help. And, hiding out didn't necessarily mean she'd done anything to deserve trouble coming her way. He wasn't as inclined as Shane to give her the third degree, although he did wish he could figure out why she looked so familiar.

"She'll tell us why she's here in good time, but until then you'll treat her with respect, Shane. And, you will not question her, you hear?"

Cade didn't wait to hear Shane's response. Laura must have heard their conversation, because the front door slammed and Cade saw their beautiful houseguest hurrying down the walkway he'd paved for Mama, backpack slung over her shoulder, blond hair swinging out behind her.

"We've got a runner," Cade said as he shoved away from the window and headed for the front door. Shane caught up to him, but Mama only made it as far as the front porch. She'd need her wheelchair or help from one of them to make it any further.

"Wait here, Shane," Cade said as he moved to catch up to the woman. Shane didn't listen, of course. He chased down their guest, and Cade saw what was about to happen a split second too late. Much too late to stop it.

Cade knew Shane meant her no harm. He only meant

to talk to her, but Shane didn't see the things Cade did. Shane didn't realize this wasn't a woman you could touch casually in that way, at least not when she felt threatened and wanted to leave. Before Cade could stop his brother, Shane reached out to grab her arm.

What he saw next was predictable to him, but it broke his heart just the same. The woman dropped to the ground, crouched over, hands on her head to ward off blows she didn't realize would never come while she was safe on their ranch. Crouched to protect herself from whatever she imagined was about to come. The sight was heart wrenching.

Shane stood over her, looking stricken, and Cade could hear Mama's concerned questions from the porch behind him. Cade moved alongside Shane. "Go on back up to the house," he said quietly, calmly. "Help Mama get lunch on the table. We'll be up soon."

Shane didn't argue this time. His face was a mask of stunned mollification as he turned back toward the porch and left Cade and Laura alone.

Laura was mortified. She moved her hands down from around her head, but used them to cover her face and the heat she knew would be in her cheeks. She knew she looked like an idiot. She squeezed her eyes shut and breathed deeply in an effort to keep tears from falling though they burned behind her lids.

By the time she'd gotten to the ranch, she was on her very last legs, tired in a way she'd never been before. Perhaps part of that was the pregnancy, but she'd had no idea how badly the exhaustion would affect her ability to cope. One minute, she'd heard Shane talking about who she was and what trouble she might bring with her and the next, she'd known she needed to get out of there. She had to go before he started asking questions she didn't want to answer. All of her usual defense mechanisms and coping tricks had left her when she'd heard the men coming up behind her. And when Shane had reached for her, she'd reacted to protect herself, her baby.

Now she was on the ground in an embarrassing display of stupidity and foolishness. Patrick's voice hissed in her ear. *Fool. Get up off the floor, Laura. They'll know what an idiot you are. Always showing your background. Always showing those damn roots.*

She could almost see him looking down at her as she crouched on the ground.

Laura didn't need Patrick's voice to tell her how stupid she looked right now. She knew it well enough herself. What would they think of her? She stayed where she was, kneeling on the ground, her face buried in her hands, making sure no tears fell to the ground. She couldn't bring herself to face anyone after that little display. Her heart beat too quickly in her chest and she needed to calm herself.

Laura heard a soft voice behind her and heard footsteps walking back toward the house. She slid one hand to the side and saw Cade sit down next to her, arms draped casually over his drawn up knees. He kept his body angled toward the barn and didn't reach out to her.

"We'll just stay here a bit. When you're ready to get up, you reach out for my arm and I'll help you up, okay?" Cade said.

Then, much to Laura's surprise, he simply talked. He didn't ask questions or try to figure out why she'd fallen to the ground and covered herself like the town idiot after a harmless touch. He didn't make a big deal out of the fact that she was practically curled in a ball. He talked about nothing and everything all at once.

"I've always loved this time of day. Come to think of it, I

52

love any time of day, but this time is especially nice. Middle of the day, after morning chores are done: animals fed, stalls cleaned, all turned out to pasture. After lunch, I've got nothing but playtime to look forward to. Ride a few of the horses. Do some training with my girl, Red."

Cade's voice was soothing, calming. A balm somehow on her frazzled nerves. He spoke as though he expected nothing from her, and that in itself was comforting.

"Hey, speak of the devil herself," Cade said. There was a spark of genuine pleasure to his voice that drew Laura's head up a bit.

When she lifted her head, she was face to face with a beautiful red dog wagging her tail, low and fast. The dog sniffed the air in Laura's direction as if trying to get a reading of some sort, and her whole body wriggled as she came forward and licked at Laura's hands. Hands that shook as they reached out, unsure of herself but drawn to the beautiful creature in front of her.

The dog's eyes were warm and deep and she let Laura pet behind her silken ears. The muscles that rippled beneath the dog's short hair spoke of power and strength, but she was gentle and timid, almost as if she saw something familiar in Laura and wanted to connect with her.

"Well, I'll be. She really likes you," Cade said with a laugh.

Laura looked over to see him watching as Red continued to wriggle under Laura's pats and scratches.

"She didn't let me touch her until today. It took me about four weeks to earn that, and here you are on the farm for an hour and she waltzes up, pretty as a picture, and lets you snuggle with her. Ms. Red, I don't mind telling you, I'm feeling a little like a jilted lover."

A smile tugged at the corners of Laura's mouth. He still

hadn't pressed her for answers or tried to lure her back inside. Laura looked over at his kind green eyes that watched as she petted Red. If she didn't get up soon, she'd either lose feeling in her legs or fall back in the dirt. With a deep fortifying breath, Laura reached out and took hold of Cade's arm. Cade simply smiled and helped pull her to her feet. They walked inside together as if he'd only taken her for a tour of the ranch before lunch.

CHAPTER EIGHT

Cade and May carried on an easy conversation during lunch, talking about the animals on the ranch, the new scholarship Shane was setting up for her, Red's progress with people, and more. Shane sat quietly as if he didn't know what to say to Laura, and Laura focused only on avoiding eye contact with everyone. Between Cade and May's conversation, the air didn't hang near as heavy as it could have.

"Did you get José the papers to renew their lease, Shane?" May asked her oldest son.

Shane nodded and swallowed a mouthful of food. "We signed everything last week. I wrote up a twenty-five year lease this time so we don't have to worry about it for a while, but I gave him a clause to get out of it if he needs to."

"Good," May said then turned to Laura. "The ranch is four thousand acres, but we don't use all of that anymore. We use about five hundred acres for the animals Cade rehabs, but we lease the other thirty-five hundred acres to José Sandoval and his family. They own a small plot behind us that was too small to do much with. By leasing our land, they're able to turn a profit on their cattle. You may see the cattle as they're rotated through the different pastures from time to time. José and his wife often come over for dinner on Sundays, and they help us out around here when we need them."

Laura nodded. Later, she would wonder why they didn't use the land themselves anymore. For now, she was too distracted to think about anything other than whether staying on the ranch was a good idea. She needed to rest for a day or two, but should probably move on after that.

Maybe she could get in touch with John Smith and have him send the permanent identity to her here before relocating. But would staying that long be wise? It would be a few weeks, at least. It didn't seem like a good idea to just sit and wait for the Kensingtons to track her down.

No. I'd better move on and have him send it to me down the road somewhere.

Laura was lost in thought when May's voice pulled her back to the present. "My husband was always more interested in his inventions than in running the ranch," May said, with a wistful smile. "His family had worked it for generations, but he liked tinkering in the barn more than he liked keeping cattle in it. For years we all teased him about it."

Cade and Shane shared a wry smile as Laura looked from one of them to the other, trying to understand.

Shane sounded a little bitter when he explained. "It wasn't always easy trying to run the ranch while he was busy with his inventing, but in the end, the joke was on all of us. He invented an industrial glue, pretty much by accident one day. I'm still not sure what he was trying to invent that day. But the glue is what came out. It's used in manufacturing all over the world now. The patent earned him enough money to play in his tinker barn, as we call it, until the day he died and beyond."

Laura smiled, but she didn't miss the way a little of the light left May's expression at the mention of her husband's passing. May and her husband must have been truly in love. That was what Laura had hoped for herself one day. It seemed like a lifetime ago that she'd dared to dream of love, but in reality had only been three years.

"Well boys, go on and get this table cleared so you can get back to work."

Laura almost did a double take as the men rose without complaint and began clearing the table. Patrick would never have helped with what he saw as a woman's work.

"Aren't lawyers supposed to have days packed full of appointments and meetings?" May chided Shane as he piled the plates in a stack to clear them.

"Not small-town lawyers, Mama," he answered, but Laura could hear affection in his voice, not genuine correction.

Laura moved to help clear the dishes away but May insisted she sit and relax.

"You rest some more and then I'll show you to your room after the boys go back to work. You can settle in."

Laura blanched. *Settle in.* She had no idea where she would go or how she would find a job, but she couldn't possibly stay here for more than a day or so. She couldn't shake the feeling that she needed to keep moving, keep running.

"I'll begin looking for work and a place to stay right away," she started, thinking she'd just tell them she had found work and move along, but May cut her off.

"You'll do no such thing. Josh knew what he was doing when he sent you here. And, if he sent you to me, I'm guessing you've got no family to take you in and no job prospects. It'll be wonderful to have some company around here during the day."

Laura could tell Cade and Shane were listening. Their conversation had quieted in the other room, but they didn't argue with their mother's offer.

"Now then," May said as she pushed herself up from the table, "let me show you your room." With that, she moved toward the stairs and made her way up, leaning heavily on the railing, clearly expecting Laura to follow.

Laura didn't know what to say or do. If Patrick's family found her here, she could bring trouble to the Bishops. She couldn't do that to them.

She weighed her options, and there weren't many. She'd worked at a diner as a waitress in high school. It wouldn't be fun to be on her feet for ten-hour shifts when she got further along in her pregnancy, but plenty of women had done it. She'd do it, too.

After a few days' rest at the ranch, she'd slip out and move on to look for work and a quiet place to settle. Maybe she could call Josh and see if he could get her money from the greenhouse and wire it to her. If she left as soon as she received the wire, she wouldn't be around for the Kensingtons to catch up to her. That would give her enough to put down a deposit on an apartment in a new place.

Laura rose and started up the stairs after May, who moved painstakingly slowly. Shane came into the room, hands shoved in his pockets. Cade stood behind him. He cleared his throat and Laura paused.

"Laura. I um, I just want you to know, I won't say anything. What I mean is, you'll be safe here," Shane said, eyes on the floor. "We won't tell anyone you're here."

Laura swallowed past the lump in her throat and

nodded before turning up the stairs again. She knew she should tell them that her husband was dead, that his family might be coming after her. That maybe her husband had been in some sort of trouble before he died. The needles of doubt pegged her again when she thought of the USB drive she'd left hidden in the kitchen.

She should tell them about the baby. But she couldn't bring herself to tell them any of it. Laura pushed aside the guilt that swirled around her and followed May upstairs. With any luck, she was overreacting. Whatever Patrick had been involved in, whatever he'd hidden, was nothing that could come back to haunt her. With any luck, the Kensingtons would let her go and she'd live in peace, finally free of her husband and the horror her life had become the last few years.

CHAPTER NINE

Alec Hall rested his hand on the ornate wrought-iron railing leading to Martha Kensington's Upper West Side brownstone. Over the past two days, he'd been by the side of his deceased business partner's mother and brother, helping with the funeral arrangements. He'd ensured that the newspapers and news stations had photos of Patrick Kensington that had been approved by Martha, and patiently bided his time. He'd have to put up this façade as long as necessary to find the evidence he hadn't known existed until it was too late. He needed to get into Patrick's home and search for the proof Patrick had threatened him with in his dying moments.

He had no idea if the evidence would be on paper, on a thumb drive, or on Patrick's computer. Hell, it could be anything and anywhere. But no matter its form, he needed to find it before someone else did.

Alec was tired of having to kowtow to Martha. He'd been doing that for the last ten years as Patrick's partner, and it sickened him to have to continue now. Martha didn't know the truth about his background. If she had, she never would have let her son associate with him, much less go into business with him. Martha Kensington had controlled Patrick mercilessly; she always had. If her background check into Alec had been able to get past the backstory he had created, she would know Alec was nothing more than a street kid with a long juvenile record, a kid who'd grown up as Alec Halligan in the gutters of New York City. If she'd known that, she would have put an end to Patrick's dealings with Alec right away. Kensingtons didn't mix with the Alec Halligans of the world.

Patronizing Martha a little longer was a necessity now. Alec needed access to Patrick's home and to his wife. He had to be sure Laura Kensington didn't know anything about the evidence Patrick had dug up the week before his death. The best way to do that was to stay close to the family, to be supportive, and solicitous. To cater to their every damn need, as they were accustomed to.

Justin answered his knock and ushered him in, then shut the door against the flashbulbs of the reporters who surrounded the front steps. The reporters hadn't been satisfied with the canned statements made by the family's publicist, but then again, when someone as prominent and wealthy as Patrick Kensington died, the vultures were never satisfied with scraps.

The shit I could tell them about that man.

Ironically, Patrick had never cared when Alec made sure they were awarded projects with well-placed cash gifts, or a favor here or there for someone in a position to help them. He hadn't cared when Alec had gotten a little rough on occasion to make sure other companies backed out of a project, or to ensure someone kept a promise made to him or Patrick. He hadn't cared one bit when Alec had subbed out materials on jobs to raise their profit margin. But when he'd figured out Alec was skimming a little extra for himself now and then... Well, that had been another story altogether. The pompous ass thought he could come down on Alec, threaten him with jail time and exposure. Patrick thought he'd pin all of the company's wrongdoing over the years on Alec, getting away free and clear, and getting rid of Alec in the process.

But, that wasn't happening. Alec was the one who had taken all the risks, did the dirty work to build that company. He deserved a bigger piece of the pie, so he'd taken it. And he'd be damned if he would let any of the Kensingtons take that away from him. Not Patrick, and certainly not his little mouse of a wife, Laura. He didn't know if Laura had the evidence, or even knew what had been happening. He was fairly sure Patrick wouldn't have shared anything with his wife, but who could be certain? He sure as hell wasn't taking any chances now.

"How are you holding up, Justin?" Alec asked quietly, ever playing the part. He handed his coat to the house-keeper who waited silently beside the door.

He followed Justin into the sitting room on the left and was greeted by the always-cold eyes of Martha Kensington. Justin didn't answer Alec's query; he just grunted and poured himself another drink from the sidebar then waved the bottle at Alec with a brow raised in question.

Alec nodded, accepted the drink, and sat next to Martha.

"How are you feeling, Martha? Have the reporters been at you all morning?" She would lay her son to rest today. Alec almost felt a pinch of remorse for the pain she must be going through. Just a pinch, easily pushed aside when he thought about the way Patrick had cornered him. He hadn't had any choice when it came down to it. Alec had learned

LORI RYAN

at an early age that the only way to get yourself out of a corner was to come out swinging. Swing fast and hard, and don't stop fighting until your opponent lay bleeding on the floor beneath you.

Martha's husband had died from a heart attack at the age of forty-three, and his father before him had died almost as young from heart failure. No one had questioned it when Patrick suffered the same end. He had only been thirty-seven but with a family history like that, who would think to look for poison in his system? Tox screens weren't done as a matter of course unless there was some reason to go digging, and succinylcholine wouldn't be stumbled upon unless someone found a reason to go looking. Alec knew enough about the nurse who'd given him the drug that she'd keep his secret forever, provided he did the same with hers. She no more wanted her secrets to come out than he did.

Alec didn't receive an answer from Martha either, because the phone rang as soon as the words were out of his mouth. She turned to pick it up as if she were glad to skip the obligation of conversing with him. As he listened to her side of the conversation and watched her stony eyes grow even harder, several things became clear.

First, she'd sent her driver to pick Laura up at the hospital rather than see to her daughter-in-law herself or even send Justin to bring her to their home. Typical, Alec realized. He and Laura had been treated in much the same manner: as outsiders who hadn't measured up. Not that anyone really measured up in the Kensingtons' world.

When Patrick and Laura had married three years ago, Alec wondered why his partner had married a woman who clearly didn't meet his family's standards. Laura came from the wrong side of the tracks in a small New Jersey town that Patrick liked to say was the armpit of the state. At first Alec thought Patrick was rebelling in some way, but that wasn't it at all. It hadn't taken Alec long to figure out control was the name of the game. Patrick liked the control he had over Laura, the way he could hold himself over her with such superiority.

His mother did the same thing with everyone around her, and Alec had to wonder if Laura had been paying the price for Martha's treatment of Patrick these past few years. It was ironic, really. Martha Kensington was no better a mother than Alec's own crack-whore of a mother had been. Which was to say, not very good at all. Alec suppressed a laugh at the thought and refocused on Martha's conversation.

Before Martha had even hung up the phone, Alec deciphered what had happened. Laura wasn't in the hospital or anywhere else that the driver could find. She was missing. He forced his hand to loosen around the glass he held and set it carefully on the table as Martha hung up the phone.

"She never allowed the doctor to check her in. She simply left saying her sister was picking her up. She doesn't have a sister!" Martha ranted.

Her voice was cold and tight with indignation. There was no concern for Laura or her well-being in the tone, only anger that she would dare defy Martha and her wishes.

Justin grunted and downed the rest of his drink before pouring another one.

Martha rose, her carriage regal and commanding. "Lord knows what goes through that ignorant woman's head, but I won't allow her to embarrass us in this manner." Martha handed her empty glass to Justin. "Alec, put out a statement that Laura is still under her doctor's care and not able to attend services today due to her fragile state." The words were spit out with an appropriate level of poison to their tone.

Your concern for Laura is touching, Martha.

Alec pulled out his cell phone and flipped through his contacts. "I've got the number for a private investigator I've worked with on some sensitive matters. His agency is excellent and highly regarded. He'll keep this quiet while he tracks her down."

Martha made a dismissive noise, but Alec chose to take that as assent and made the call anyway. If Laura was on the run, that only confirmed his suspicion. Patrick must have given her the evidence he had against Alec before he died. Alec needed to find her. Fast.

CHAPTER TEN

L aura followed the paved path down toward the large red barn that housed Cade's horses and a few dogs he picked up from time to time. She'd spent the morning listening to May tell her about Evers, the town closest to the Bishop Ranch. Apparently, there wasn't much more to it than what she'd seen on her way through the day before.

There was Jansen's Feed Store, a diner run by two sisters who spent most of their time arguing—but whose cooking couldn't be beat, so people put up with the bickering—a bank, gas station, and convenience store. There were a few old buildings that now housed a gallery and a potter's workshop that had begun to draw tourists on the weekends. Three churches rounded out the lot.

While May talked, Laura planned. She had almost six hundred dollars in cash left. Not really enough to buy a reliable car if she wanted to have anything left for a hotel room when she stopped to rest. She'd need to take a bus if she wanted to move again. *Big city or small town?* There was probably more opportunity to hide herself among a large number of people in a city and better odds she'd get a job right away, but the cost of living would be higher. In the end, she'd decided to look for a moderately sized city—large enough to get lost in, but small enough so the cost of living wouldn't be overwhelming. She needed to settle somewhere and let the man working on her identity know where she was so she could get her papers. She had decided to contact Josh and see if he could get to her cash in the greenhouse to send on to her wherever she settled.

After they finished making a stew that was now simmering on the stove, May had trimmed the excess fat off the meat they hadn't used, and sent Laura down to the barn with the scraps for Red. As she walked, Laura looked out over the endless fields at the horses grazing in the heat of the Texas day. There was a stillness and quiet to the ranch that calmed Laura. She knew she had to keep moving to stay safe, but she was grateful for the small respite she'd been offered here. And honestly, she had a feeling it wasn't going to be easy to move on.

She'd spent her whole life under the thumb of a cruel and unforgiving father who hated her simply for being born —and later, living in fear of her husband's fists and the cruel blows they struck with such ease. From the moment she'd discovered she was pregnant, she'd known it was only a matter of time before one of Patrick's blows would hit her in the wrong place and take her baby's life.

The ranch seemed to have an energy that whispered of possibilities to Laura. It told her she could be anything she chose to be, anyone she set out to be. She had only to decide who or what, and embrace her future. If only she wasn't afraid to listen to those whispers, afraid to believe their message. Afraid to stay in one place.

Laura looked up to see Red trotting toward her, mouth open and happy, tongue lolling as she panted in the heat.

Laura laughed and knelt down. It was amazing how easily the dog brought a smile to her face. One that was genuine and heartfelt, not forced and polite.

"Hey beautiful girl. I brought you a surprise," Laura said, pulling the chunks of meat out for a greedy mouth that gobbled them down in one bite.

"Mornin', Laura," Cade said from twenty feet away. He leaned on the barn door, shoulder against the edge, long legs crossed. He was as relaxed and in his element as any man could be. Though Cade was tall and lean, she could tell he was muscular beneath the tan work shirt and worn jeans, and Laura was embarrassed to find that her pulse quickened whenever he was near her. For a split second, she found herself wondering what it would feel like to run her hands over those muscles, to feel that strength. She pushed the urge and the thoughts away.

His dark hair fell messily over his forehead, framing green eyes that always seemed to be smiling. "It was like she heard you coming a mile away. Whined for me to open the door so she could get to you."

Cade was so unlike the men she'd met in her life so far. He didn't move toward Laura. He seemed unhurried, as if he could wait for her to choose to either walk away or toward him, without any concern over the way the decision went. Oddly, she felt a pang at the thought that he might not care if she walked away. A part of her that had been long dead wanted him to care. Wanted him to *want* her.

Laura closed the yards between them slowly, not at all sure she really wanted to spend any more time than she had to with anyone on the ranch if she was only going to leave. But she was drawn to him despite her hesitation. Red followed by her side, keeping herself in contact with Laura's leg as they walked.

"She probably just smelled the meat May sent down for her," Laura said.

She didn't know what else to say after that. She crossed her arms, holding herself in the protective bubble she'd built over the last few years. It'd been a long time since she'd talked to anyone outside her husband's family, unless you counted the polite, mindless chatter that had been expected at business functions and social events. There, she'd worn a carefully constructed mantle that showed the world what they expected to see.

Laura didn't want to step back into the persona she'd worn for the last three years as Patrick's wife. She didn't want to be that person anymore.

Cade filled in the silence for her. "I can show you the horses, introduce you to a few of them," he said, motioning over his shoulder with an easy jerk of the chin toward the barn.

Laura nodded. She followed him into the barn, but stayed back a few paces. He didn't seem to care if she talked or not, which in itself took the pressure off and made it easier to be around him.

Laura followed Cade up to one of the stall doors, but stepped back when a large brown head with a white stripe down the center popped over the half door.

"Oh!" The horse was much larger than Laura had thought it would be, making her wonder whether she really wanted to meet the magical creatures she'd seen in the fields on her way down from the house. They seemed smaller from a distance. Smaller, and safer, too.

The horse lowered his head and shoved at Cade's chest, throwing him back a foot or two and making him laugh—a rich deep laugh that seemed to reach right into Laura and warm her from the inside out.

"He's looking for a mint," Cade said, and pulled a wrapped peppermint out of his pocket. He raised a brow and looked at Laura. "You want to feed him?"

Laura frowned at the mint in Cade's hand. "You're teasing me. He doesn't eat mints," she said, looking back at the beautiful horse who continued to push at Cade for the candy.

This brought more laughter rumbling from Cade's chest. "I wouldn't tease you like that. Horses love mints. I promise. I probably shouldn't feed them as many as I do, but I can't help it. I'm a pushover." He stepped aside, giving Laura more space. She watched his face for a long moment searching for signs that he was teasing, but he seemed to be telling the truth.

She reluctantly stepped forward and eyed the mint sitting on Cade's open palm. Laura reached forward and took the candy from his hand, then watched as Cade rubbed the palm of his hand up and down the white marking on the horse's face. The horse leaned in for the rubbing, seeming to enjoy the contact.

She was mesmerized watching those large hands stroke the horse. Cade's hands had never hit a woman—of that Laura was absolutely sure. She didn't know how, but she knew it with a certainty that calmed her. His were hands that were strong and sure, but they were gentle at the same time. They healed and loved and taught, but they didn't hurt.

She took a step toward the horse, but faltered as he turned his head. He reached his nose toward her hand with lips working furiously to try to reach the mint.

"His mouth is huge," Laura said, and pulled her hand back.

"He won't hurt you. Just hold it flat on your hand and

he'll do the rest. You won't even feel his teeth, I promise." Cade slipped his hand under hers, cushioning it as she reached forward with the candy.

Cade was right. The horse's mouth was velvet on her palm as he lipped the candy off her hand. It disappeared with a satisfying crunch that lured a laugh from Laura, despite herself.

"What's his name?" she asked as she placed her hand on the flat of the horse's face as Cade had done. She was rewarded when the horse leaned in to her hand and let her rub.

"Cayenne's Pride was his racing name. Race horses have names that tell you where they came from. The Cayenne tells you what stable he was out of. He came from Cayenne Jackson's place. Pride is sort of like his given name. I can't decide if I want to call him Cayenne or Pride or come up with something totally different. Time will tell," Cade said.

"He's yours? I thought all the horses here came to be rehabbed and then rehomed."

"Most do, but I'm keeping him. My horse had to be put down about a year ago. Had bone cancer. I've been waiting for another horse to come along that spoke to me. This guy's it. I knew it the minute I saw him." Cade looked at the horse with a reverent love and respect that Laura figured was what made him so good at what he did. It took her breath away to see the relationship between the two.

"Why did he retire?" Laura asked.

"Hock injury. He's been on stall rest but I'm rehabbing him gradually. He'll be sound again soon. His injury wasn't serious enough to cause him to be lame for life, it just isn't something a racehorse owner wants to deal with. There was a time when they would've put him down, but nowadays there are people like me who take them and work with them."

Cayenne's Pride flipped his head with a neigh and drew back into the stall to pull hay from a bracket on the wall.

"I guess we've been dismissed," Cade said with a smile. "Come on, I'll show you Millie. She'll have a fit if we don't visit her."

They turned toward the other end of the barn, but footsteps behind them made Laura whirl. It had only been a day since her arrival, and she still felt as if the Kensingtons would show up any minute to take her back.

Laura took a steadying breath when she saw it was only Shane coming around the corner into the barn. He still made her jumpy, but she'd rather see him than the Kensingtons. She knew Cade watched her closely, aware of her attempt to regulate her breathing. The man saw way too much. No doubt he had read every line of tension that spiked before she'd seen Shane, and had questions about what caused her to tense up, but she wasn't ready to answer anyone's questions yet.

"Hey, Cade, Laura."

"What brings you here two days in a row, Shane?" Cade taunted. "You rethinking that career in town? I have stalls you can muck out if you're looking for a change."

Shane laughed and shook his head. "You can keep your horse sh—" He glanced at Laura, amending his sentence. "I'll let you handle the pitchfork." The brothers smiled at each other and Laura began to relax, but the feeling was short lived.

Shane's face became serious as he looked at Laura. "I actually came out to talk to you, Laura. It seems you've made the news."

She couldn't have controlled the intake of breath if she'd

tried. She felt Cade move closer to her as the muscles in her shoulders tensed so tightly they hurt. Cade didn't touch her, but she felt his presence next to her as palpably as she felt her own nails dig into the palms of her hands. Shane handed her a printout from *The New York Times* online, and she immediately recognized the picture of her standing next to Patrick on the front page. It had been taken at last year's Christmas party for Patrick's business. She'd had to wear the high-collared navy blue dress to hide the marks that marred her neck.

A headline above the picture read: Laura Kensington Missing. Laura let her eyes drop to the print and scanned the text. Most of the quotes came from her husband's business partner, a man who had always frightened Laura almost as much as Patrick had. There was an underlying evil behind the mask he wore for the world. The same way Patrick's face had always been a mask hiding the devil.

The words in the article hit her full force in the gut. Unstable, emotionally distraught after husband's death, pregnant, danger to herself or child.

The irony of it all was that Patrick and his family wouldn't have known about the baby if he'd died a week earlier.

Laura shivered as she remembered Patrick standing over her while she sat on the toilet when he'd made her take a pregnancy test. She'd already known the outcome—had for weeks. She had tried to hide it from him, but he didn't buy her excuses when she'd been vomiting daily for over two weeks.

If he hadn't caught on, if he hadn't made her take the test and then called his family to brag about the son he was sure he would have, the family would have gladly let her walk away after his death. They would be relieved to be rid of the *trash* Patrick had brought home.

Laura took a step back. The paper fell from her hands, as one hand landed on her stomach. She looked at Cade and Shane, shaking her head and moving away from them as if by sheer will she could somehow make this go away.

"It's all right, Laura," Shane said. "You don't have to leave. If there's a reason you can't go back there, the ranch is the safest place for you to be."

"No." Laura shook her head again. They now knew her secret. "I have to go. I have to leave. People have seen me here." She backpedaled further, then realized she'd worked herself into a corner. Would the Bishops question her stability now, or wonder if she'd hurt her baby after reading those lies?

Laura's mind raced to the people in town who had seen her get off the bus, to Tom Jansen and Seth who would surely recognize her. She'd need to change her appearance and get hold of another fake identity. She had to get far away from anyone who had seen her until she could change the way she looked. She needed to be sure no one could force her and her baby back to the Kensingtons.

"Laura," Cade said, quietly and calmly, stepping in front of her and leaning down to catch her gaze without touching her. He drew her eyes to his before speaking again.

"Shane didn't tell you because we want you to leave. He told you so we could help. You need to trust us, Laura. This is the safest place for you to be. Even if anyone other than Shane happens to read *The New York Times*." Cade threw a wry glance over his shoulder at Shane before looking back to Laura as though he didn't understand why his brother would read a national paper in their small town. "No one that's seen you will tell anyone where you are. People around here are loyal to a fault to Mama. She's helped all of them, one way or another, and sent half the kids around here to college or trade school or something. If people know May Bishop is protecting you, you're as safe as you can be. I promise."

Shane stepped up behind Cade. "He's right, Laura. No one's going to tell anyone you're here. And with Cade here, no one's going to be able to get on the grounds and get to you without him knowing it. If you leave, you'll be out there on your own."

Laura didn't need him to tell her that. She knew better than anyone if she ran from the ranch she was heading out into nothing, with no one to support her. Still, what choice did she have? What if she brought trouble to these people? There was trouble coming for her one way or another. Whether it was in the form of the Kensingtons coming after her for the baby or someone else coming because of what-ever had put fear into Patrick's eyes before his death, she didn't know. But she knew trouble would come before long.

"Laura, no." Cade's voice was quiet with the command he issued so calmly. A command urging her not to run.

She felt Red press against her legs as if she too had something to say about the situation.

Cade's voice changed to a plea. "Let's go on up and talk to Mama."

"You don't have to go back to the house," came May's voice from behind the men. "I'm here. Joelle called and told me she saw the article in the paper. She read me the whole thing." May rolled her wheelchair further into the barn and Laura let her gaze meet the woman's sharp eyes. "Unstable my foot. What a load of nonsense. You'd think a reputable newspaper like that would have the decency to check some facts before printing rubbish. Now then, when the baby gets here, you'll need a little more room. Cade, let's move Laura's things into the room at the back of the house. There's a small bedroom that connects to it through a shared bathroom, Laura. When the baby comes, you'll be nice and close but still have plenty of space to yourself."

The fact that Laura hadn't told them, wasn't even showing yet, and the baby wouldn't be arriving for months, didn't seem to faze May.

Laura looked back at Cade and Shane and shook her head. "I can't stay, May. If they find me, they'll take the baby. Martha Kensington won't let me raise what she sees as her family, her blood."

She didn't mention the USB drive hidden in her kitchen. She wouldn't open up about all her secrets, no matter how trustworthy these people seemed.

May didn't answer. She spoke to her sons instead. "Boys, go on up to the house and get the other room ready. Laura and I are going to talk."

"Yes, ma'am," Cade said as he and Shane headed toward the house.

May wheeled herself next to a stack of hay bales and patted one. "Sit, Laura."

Laura wasn't sure what had just happened. May's force seemed undeniable. When she rolled into the barn and started giving orders, it was hard not to follow them. She walked to the hay bale and sat, eyeing May with a wary gaze. Part of her wanted May and the boys to be right—to convince her that staying on the ranch would keep her safe.

"Tell me, Laura. Do you have anyone you can go to? Any family to help or friends you can stay with?"

Laura squeezed her eyes shut and shook her head. She opened her eyes and let her gaze meet May's. "I need to keep moving. Change my appearance. Use a different name."

How could I have been so stupid to tell people my name was Laura? I didn't even try to hide my appearance. How will I take care of a child if I'm not even smart enough to disguise myself the right way?

May's eyes fell to Laura's hands, once again on her stomach. It was odd really. At this stage of her pregnancy, Laura wasn't showing and she couldn't even feel the baby yet. She had nothing physical to go on other than the word of her doctor and the constant exhaustion and nausea she felt every day. Yet, somehow, she felt the need to cradle and protect it even though she couldn't feel or see it. The baby was as real to her already as if she held it in her hands.

May nodded slowly, as if she were thinking. "I thought that might be the case. Seth's going to bring Joelle over in the morning. She hasn't worked in years, but she was a damn good hairdresser once upon a time. She'll give you a haircut, and she says she has a hair dye that'll darken your hair to a light brown but is safe for the baby."

Laura's hand flew to her hair. "I'm not allowed to—" She clamped her mouth shut as she realized what she'd been about to say. She had never been allowed to cut her hair. Patrick liked it long.

May didn't miss a beat. Just pretended the statement had never been made. "She'll be here in the morning. After that, you can decide if you want to keep moving. But, I'll tell you this, Laura. I think you need to take a chance on us. I think you need to stay and let us keep you safe here."

Laura raised her chin. "I can't bring trouble to your door. It might put you and Cade in danger if I stay here." Laura ignored the mental flash of Cade's muscular stature that hit her, evidence of his ability to protect himself.

May dismissed her concern with a wave of her hand. "Cade won't let anything happen to us, Laura. You're safe here, and so are we."

She patted the handles of her wheelchair. "Now, push me back on up the walk and we'll get lunch on the table. My arms get real tired pushing this chair back, even with the paved walk. That hill is brutal."

CHAPTER ELEVEN

Alec opened the door and let the two private investigators into the foyer. He'd already received a phone report from them, and knew they hadn't found any sign of Laura Kensington. It was the lack of any clues to her whereabouts that prompted the call to the press to get the word out about her disappearance. It had been his stroke of genius to include the information about her tenuous mental state and her pregnancy. She'd be brought home quickly once people found out she was desperately in need of care and assistance. That's the kind of thing people did for the Kensingtons. The national papers had picked up the story and run with it faster than he'd even imagined they would.

The investigators followed Alec into the sitting room where Martha and Justin waited. Alec still hadn't figured out if Justin would be an asset or not in this whole screwed up situation. Alec knew Justin and Patrick weren't very close, but even so, Justin seemed to want to find Laura. That desire could prove helpful.

"Martha, Justin, these are the two investigators I told you about. Mark Sanders and Paul Cummings. They've run checks on Laura's credit cards and she hasn't used them at all. They've talked to the hospital staff but they're being extremely tight-lipped so far. The doctor you spoke with told us she refused to be checked in. She said her sister would pick her up and she left. We can officially report Laura missing today and get the police involved, but I'd still like to keep Mark and Paul on the payroll so we have our own men looking for her," Alec said.

"Can't you just get videos or whatever from the hospital and see who picked her up? Which way she went? Who she was with? Little hussy was probably having an affair." Martha sniffed as though just talking about her daughter-in-law was distasteful to her.

"We're using inside connections to see if we can get video footage at the hospital, ma'am, but it's not easy. The privacy regulations in place nowadays make it hard for us to get things like that. What we need from you right now..."

Alec cringed as Mark continued to talk. Calling Martha Kensington 'ma'am' was one strike against him. Telling her what to do would be a second strike. But Mark just continued on as though he didn't see the pinched expression on Martha's face.

"What we need from both you and your son right now are as many details about Laura as you can tell us. Who are her friends? What are her hobbies? Where does she spend time during the day? Does she belong to any clubs or organizations? Go to any meetings or classes or social events routinely? Who would she contact if she wanted someone to console her?" Mark asked.

Paul stood behind Mark, pen in hand, ready to take notes. He'd be waiting a long time. Alec was willing to bet Laura didn't have any friends here, and even if she did, Martha probably hadn't deigned to pay attention to her life.

He'd also bet Justin wasn't around often enough to know a damned thing.

"I'm not really sure who she spent time with. Laura spent a lot of her time keeping my brother's calendar for him. I know that. She was very good at it. I'm not sure what she did when she wasn't taking care of the house or Patrick." Justin looked at his mother for a lifeline.

She didn't provide one.

"Gentlemen, I am not my daughter-in-law's keeper. I don't know what she did with her time," Martha said, that cold tone creeping into her voice to let the men know her patience was waning.

Mark's eyes flicked to Alec for a second. "Can you think of any friends she had that we can talk to? Any bit of information right now would be helpful."

Before Alec could answer, Martha spoke up. "She didn't have any friends that I ever met. She was very quiet; kept to herself. That's all I can tell you. But that doesn't change anything. That girl has no right taking my grandchild away from me, and she's sadly mistaken if she thinks she's going to raise that baby. That baby is a Kensington and it will be raised by Kensingtons."

"Mother, that's a ridiculously archaic view. It's her baby as much as it was Patrick's," Justin said.

Martha shrugged as though she didn't intend to listen to him at all.

"Mark, Paul, why don't you wait outside for me. I'll just be a few more minutes," Alec said and waited until the investigators left before continuing. "Martha, I'm not sure you'll be able to get custody of the baby even if we do find Laura." Alec needed to find out exactly what Martha planned and decide how to use that to his advantage. "Getting custody may be extremely difficult."

If looks could kill... Martha clearly didn't appreciate his take on things.

"Money buys anything, Alec." Martha shot a look to Justin as she spoke, shutting down whatever he had been about to say as well. "I've got nothing but money and influence, and I intend to use it. That woman will not raise a Kensington." Justin cursed as Martha walked out of the room as calmly as if she'd simply told the help what she wanted served for dinner that evening.

"Sorry, Alec. I'm fairly sure she thinks this is the nineteen-fifties, and she'll be able to have Laura hidden away in a hospital or something while she keeps the baby. Either that or she plans to pay off a judge. I'm hoping we can find Laura and talk her into coming back to have the baby here. Maybe if she's nearby and lets us be a part of her life, I can keep my mother from doing something insane."

Alec had to fight the urge to roll his eyes. Justin apparently hadn't a clue what Laura had been through at the hands of his brother, or he wouldn't glibly suggest she might let his family be a part of the baby's life. It was almost sad how dysfunctional this family was. They'd been handed everything, and this is what they'd become. If Alec had had only half or a quarter of what they'd had growing up... He shook his head. On second thought, he wouldn't have wanted it. If he had grown up like this, he might be as soft and spineless as the man in front of him. Alec wouldn't want that for all the ease and money in the world.

Alec cleared his throat. "I'll need the key to Patrick's house. We should look and see if she left any clues that might lead to her whereabouts." *And search for any evidence that needs to be destroyed along with Laura Kensington.*

"Yeah, sure. I'll get it for you." Justin stood and began to leave, only to turn back. "Look, Alec, I know she comes off as a hard-ass," he said, looking in the direction his mother had gone, "but losing Patrick is killing her. And, to have Laura run off with his baby is just too much."

Alec nodded. He didn't believe there was a damn thing that could hurt Martha Kensington. She wanted that baby because she saw it as a possession, a pawn in some bizarre game she was playing—nothing more. He'd play along, he'd use the considerable sway and resources of the Kensington family to track down Laura but he'd be damned if that baby was ever going to be born. He'd see to it that Laura had a tragic accident or decided to take her own life as soon as she was found. There wasn't any other way to be sure his secrets were never revealed.

CHAPTER TWELVE

Cade and Shane hadn't been kidding when they said the ranch would be a safe place for Laura. It seemed the whole town somehow knew who she was, but they also seemed to know she couldn't go back to the Kensingtons. For whatever reason, everyone was willing to protect her, though no one knew all of the facts surrounding her decision to hide.

Joelle cut Laura's hair into a shoulder-length, wind-blown style and used a dye that turned her almost white-blond hair golden brown. With the changes, it made it much harder to recognize Laura's face as that of Patrick Kensington's infamous wife, now plastered on every news channel and in every newspaper.

Yesterday, Nancy Wills and Tammy Cash—two women from town that were Laura's age and friends with Cade and Shane—came over with two boxes of old clothes for Laura. They brought some that would fit now and some things that would fit as she got further along in her pregnancy, which was a relief, given that she'd been wearing the few things Josh had bought for her over and over.

She promised the women she'd have coffee with them sometime soon. Of course, that meant she'd have to leave the cloister of the ranch where she felt relatively safe. Opening herself up to the exposure of the outside world might take a while, and Laura was still undecided about staying. One day she thought she could stay and hide and feel secure on the ranch. The next, she panicked and felt the need to keep moving, to avoid settling in any one place for too long. That wasn't even taking into account that it felt wrong to simply stay and live off these people's generosity.

For now, she followed the path down to the barn to help Cade with the animals, wanting to feel as though she were contributing something, instead of just freeloading. As usual, Red came out of the barn and ran to greet Laura before she got halfway there. Cade appeared next and raised his hand in greeting but let her walk to him.

Cade was the exact opposite of Patrick, from looks to personality. He was dark haired where Patrick's hair had been light. Laura had thought Patrick was so good looking when she met him. She'd been swept away by the blond hair and blue eyes, the dimpled smile and *GQ* style that seemed to come so easily to him. It had amazed her how ugly his face could turn when he twisted it up with anger, or sneered at her when he thought she was "showing her background," as he was so fond of telling her.

Cade's face was handsome in a rugged sort of way. He always seemed to have a day's worth of growth on his jaw, and his green eyes never stopped smiling. He was relaxed and so at ease with himself. Laura wondered if that came from working with the animals. If all the unconditional love he was surrounded by all day fed his soul in a way others didn't get to experience.

She had been a horribly bad judge of character with

Patrick, but she didn't think she was being fooled by Cade. There was something about him that told her she would never need to cower around him, never need to run in fear or walk on eggshells, or wonder when the next blow would come. He'd never throw her down a flight of stairs or step on her hand, when she finally fell from the battering he was dishing out, just to see how long it would take to make her cry out in pain. He'd never drag her by the hair out to the back shed and lock her in when she didn't give him the answer he wanted to some inane question about something she couldn't even remember now.

Laura knew deep down that Cade's hands had never been raised in anger against someone weaker than him or used as weapons to hurt or lash out.

"Hey, wanna see something really cool?" Cade asked, leaning against the door and smiling.

Laura nodded and followed him into the barn and down the center aisle to the tack room at the end. He opened the door and stood back to let her look inside, giving her a wide berth. She tipped her head and leaned in to look. In the back corner lay a white cat. She had patches of tiger-patterned fur across her back and over one eye, but what was most noticeable was her very large bulging stomach.

Laura gasped and turned to Cade. "Is she pregnant?"

"Yup," Cade said, his grin huge as they stood and watched the future mother from a distance. "We should have kittens soon. She wandered in here and made herself a bed out of some old blankets. She doesn't want me near her yet, but hopefully that'll change over time."

He withdrew and sat on one of the bales of hay in the center aisle. Red climbed into his lap and snuggled in for ear scratches while Laura perched on a tack trunk across the aisle, drawing her knees up and wrapping her arms around them.

"She may always be feral, but if we feed her and care for her, maybe she'll let us near the kittens so we can socialize them. We'll get her spayed and then let her stay as a barn cat if she wants to," Cade said, smiling at Red as he spoke.

"How do you do that?" Laura asked, nodding at Red. "I mean, how do you teach them to trust you?"

Cade shrugged. "Just patience and time."

Laura watched as he rubbed Red's belly with long, slow strokes that put the dog to sleep in his lap. She was a big dog, so sleeping in his lap really amounted to trying to get as much of her body across him as she could. She hung off on both sides, head lolling happily and her back half stretched across the hay bale on the other side.

Cade didn't seem to mind her size as he continued to rub her and Laura found herself jealous of the dog for a split second. He looked up at Laura and continued. "You back off when she tells you to back off. You wait patiently, give her the space she needs when it becomes more than she can handle. And you always make sure she has a way to get out, to end the interaction if she wants to." Cade lifted his hands for a few seconds, giving Red the option to move. She snuggled deeper, so his hands went back to work.

"I don't sneak up on her. I say her name before I touch her, let her come to me instead of reaching for her. Little things like that." Cade shrugged, like it was nothing to gain the trust of a dog that had been mistreated.

Laura felt her eyes go wide as she realized he did the same things around her.

"What's that look for?" Cade asked, raising a brow.

"That's what you do with me, isn't it? You always say

something from far enough away that I know you're coming. You stay still until I come toward you." Laura could see it easily now and she shook her head. "You've been training me! Like a dog."

He just laughed. "It's just a habit, Laura. It's not something I do on purpose, now." He raised his hand up as if swearing an oath. "I promise. I haven't at any point thought of you as a dog or set out to treat you like one. Scout's honor."

Cade's comment sent her thoughts in a completely different direction. She was suddenly painfully aware that she wanted him to see her as a woman. How totally inappropriate was that? She was pregnant with her dead husband's child and running from his family. She might be a grown woman but the fact was, she'd never been independent. She'd always been tied to a man—first her father and then her husband. This was the time in her life when she needed to take charge, learn to support herself, and be independent. Yet here she was thinking about how gorgeous the man sitting across from her was, and wondering if he liked what he saw when he looked at her.

Cade frowned at her. "What are you thinking? You seem like you took a little trip in your head for a minute."

If only you knew.

Laura shook her head. She needed to figure out how she was going to take care of her baby when it came, how she would support them both. How she was going to get away from the Kensingtons and their powerful, seemingly endless, reach. How she'd fight them if they tracked her down and tried to take her baby from her. The last thing she should be thinking was what it would be like to be in Cade's arms, to touch him and feel his mouth on her skin....

"I was just thinking that I need to find a way to support myself and the baby. I can't live off you guys forever."

"Try telling that to Mama. I think she's planning to adopt you," said Cade.

Laura felt a sharp pain at his joke and had a feeling she probably grimaced. What would it have been like to be born to May Bishop? To have been raised in a place like this by someone who loved her? To receive the unconditional love that a parent is supposed to have for their child?

Fairy tales… She'd given up on things like that a long time ago. It wasn't useful to sit and pity herself and cry about her circumstances. But, being so close to a family like the Bishops made her want to go back in time and rewrite her story. If not rewrite who she was born to, at least change her decision to marry Patrick.

"Well, I'll have to come up with something," Laura said, but in all honesty waiting tables was about the only thing she was qualified to do.

She forced a smile. She may not have had a mother like May Bishop, but she'd make damn sure her child did. Her baby would know she was loved no matter what. That nothing could ever take her mother's love away. If Laura was sure of one thing in her life, she was sure of that. She would love this child with all her heart and all that she was.

"What do you like to do?" Cade asked, as if the answer to her problems was as simple as that.

She frowned. Her life had revolved first around feeding her father and keeping his house, and later keeping Patrick's schedule and meeting the social demands of being one of the Kensingtons. She had no real skills she could use to get a job.

My greenhouse.

"I like to grow things. I like the way you can tell how

healthy and alive the plants are in a greenhouse by how much chatter you can hear from them when you walk in. If they're healthy and well cared for, they talk to you the second you walk in and the hum is almost deafening." Laura glanced at Cade and was surprised to see he actually looked like he understood, like he didn't think she was crazy or stupid for thinking her plants spoke to her.

"Then that's what you should do. We'll come up with a way for you to make a living growing things," he said and shoved himself up off the bale. "Let's go see if Mama has lunch ready yet. I'm starved."

Laura felt a smile tug at the corners of her mouth. One thing she'd noticed around here was Cade sure didn't miss a meal.

CHAPTER THIRTEEN

"It's been almost two weeks, damn it. How the hell can one woman evade you for two weeks? She's got to be here somewhere!" Alec yelled into the phone after Mark finished his report. They'd found nothing. Not a damn thing.

The same not-a-damn-thing Alec had found when he'd searched Patrick and Laura's house. If Patrick had collected evidence of Alec's creative accounting measures and the bribes he'd paid to win the contracts they'd been awarded over the years, it wasn't anywhere in the house. That only left Laura. She had to have it. And, that meant he needed to have her.

"Go see that doctor again. Press him. There must be something there. And pay whatever the hell you have to for the damn security tapes from the hospital. Someone will sell them to you. There's a price for everything. Find their price!"

Alec slammed down the phone. Where the hell was Laura Kensington hiding? He threw his coffee mug across the office where it hit the wall, leaving a gouge in the plaster he'd have to find some way to cover. *Great. One more thing to take care of.*

LAURA LEANED the basket of vegetables on her hip and carried them into the house. Helping May in her garden was turning out to be as relaxing as working in her greenhouse. More so, in fact, since she and May could now cook what they had grown together. She'd never seen a Japanese eggplant, but May assured her she would love the way it thickened the pasta sauce they would make with it.

"Those look beautiful, Laura," May said as she picked up the tomatoes and green beans and placed them by the sink to wash. "We'll have to can some of these tomatoes. Have you ever canned fruits and vegetables?"

Laura shook her head as she got out the cutting board and a knife.

"It's actually silly that we call it canning, since we'll use jars, but I'll teach you how to do it." May leveled Laura with a look. "Before you move on, I mean."

This time Laura nodded, not quite knowing what to say. She knew May didn't want her to leave, and part of her was beginning to wonder if perhaps she could stay. No, *wonder,* wasn't the right word.

Hope.

But she'd learned hope hurts.

Hope. Hurt. Hope. Hurt. It was like a singsong cadence in Laura's head that wouldn't stop. Hope leads to hurt and Laura didn't want to hurt anymore. She'd hurt enough.

"You know, Laura. It occurred to me that before you leave it might be a good idea for you to talk to me about what happened to you." May said it casually, as if she were asking about the weather outside.

Laura's hands stilled but she didn't reply. She stood frozen. The idea of talking about what Patrick had done to her was absolutely mortifying. How could she tell anyone? How could she ever share those details?

"You'll be moving on soon, I suppose, so it would be like having a get-out-of-jail-free card. You get to tell someone about your time with your husband, but you don't have to worry about the repercussions. You don't have to worry about what I might think or how I'll view you because of what you tell me. You can just get it off your chest before you go."

May went on washing vegetables and handing them to Laura to cut up as if she hadn't just opened an enormous can of worms. She continued to talk, explaining the way she had prepped the raised beds for the lettuce she grew, and told Laura she'd show her where the composter was to put the scraps in. So much like her son, just talking about everyday stuff until Laura somehow let down her walls.

Before Laura knew what had happened, she had tears running down her face and she'd stopped cutting. She moved blindly to the kitchen table and sank into a chair. May just waited, chopping and stirring and adding things to a pot on the stove. She handed Laura a dish towel for her tears, before she turned back to the stove once more as if nothing were happening behind her.

"I didn't love him. Not even before I knew what he was, I mean. He was older than me, but he was attractive and paid so much attention to me. It was flattering to have someone like him pay so much attention to me. He seemed sweet and caring and he was going to take me away from my dad, which, well—that was a good thing." Laura dabbed at her cheeks with the towel, but the tears were replaced with fresh ones so quickly, it had no real effect.

"My brother saw what Patrick really was. He knew somehow and tried to tell me. He tried to convince me to move in with him and we'd share a house together, but neither one of us had a job that paid much. I was waitressing and he was working at a hardware store stocking shelves. Neither of us had gone to college. I thought if I didn't weigh him down with trying to take care of me he might put himself through community college someday. I thought Patrick might send me.... But I shouldn't have married a man I didn't love. I shouldn't have done that just to get out of the situation I was in."

She blew out a deep breath, and it felt as though some of the humiliation and pain of her marriage left her with it. "My dad threatened to disown me if I married Patrick, although I've never really been sure why. He used to tell me how worthless I was, how useless a girl was to him. But, I think he didn't want me to marry Patrick because it meant he'd need someone else to cook and clean for him—or he'd have to learn to do it himself. Of course, his threat only made the thought of marrying Patrick all the more appealing."

May came and sat with Laura at the table and held her hand while she talked. "I was so stupid," Laura all but whispered, then just stayed like that for a long time, letting the tears clean away a little bit of the pain.

"When did it start?" May prompted, not addressing whether Laura had been stupid or foolish or just naive. Laura looked at her through the tears. She never thought she'd tell the details of her life with Patrick to anyone. It was too humiliating. She didn't want people to see her as the kind of woman who would let someone do that to her, even though that's exactly what she was. Exactly what she'd become.

"On our honeymoon. He couldn't, um...when we tried to..." Laura waved her hands. "You know. When we tried, well, he couldn't. He flew into a rage. I'd never seen anything like it. He told me it was my fault, that it was me. I was a virgin. I didn't know what I was supposed to do."

"It wasn't your fault. You know that, don't you?" May asked.

Laura nodded, but didn't look at the older woman. "He hit me." Laura's hand went to her neck at the memory of that night. "Choked me."

Laura wasn't crying any longer. She stared at a scratch on the big oak table, remembering the way hitting her had gotten Patrick excited, the way he'd raped her as dark spots swam at the corner of her eyes. "Raped me," she whispered to herself.

She looked up at May. "The funny thing is, not all abusive husbands apologize the next day. You always read that, don't you? How they send flowers and apologize and tell their wives it won't ever happen again? It's not true. Patrick didn't care. He wasn't sorry. He never sent flowers or tried to make it up to me. It was just who he was."

As she spoke, the stories began to flow, coming more and more easily.

"In the beginning, he was very careful not to hit me in the face. He didn't leave marks I couldn't cover with long sleeves or a turtleneck. As time went on, his anger seemed to spiral and he wasn't able to keep things as controlled any longer. There were times when I couldn't leave the house for days."

May listened while Laura told her more than she ever thought she'd share with anyone. Her brother's death, and the resulting beating when she wanted to cancel a business dinner to go to the funeral. The way Patrick would drag her down the steps by her hair or throw her against the wall so hard the house shook. What it felt like to have a hot pan held against her skin when she didn't cook the right thing for dinner.

She told about the sick games he'd play where she'd have to go get whatever it was he wanted to hit her with. She'd have to get him his belt or the length of hose he was fond of using. And the sick thing was, she'd know whether he would rape her after or not by how the beating went. When she had to get something he'd use to hit her with, it always ended with sex. As if the beating was foreplay for him.

Sitting at May's kitchen table, Laura let out years of grief and anger and guilt and self-doubt. Everything came pouring out of her. Her plan to run. Her hope to keep her baby safe. It all came pouring out until there were no more words. There was nothing more to do than let May hold her and rock her, and as she sat there in May's arms she began to let go of three years of absolute terror.

CHAPTER FOURTEEN

Shane stood at the bottom of a ladder in their dad's old barn in an unused pasture behind the house. They called the building their father's "Tinker Barn" because he'd filled it with work benches and shelves and tools and places to tinker. It still stood even though his father had been gone for years.

He called up to Cade a second time but got no answer. Tinny music blared through the speakers of the radio Cade had had since they were teenagers. How that thing still worked, Shane didn't know. He could also hear the sound of Cade's fists hitting one of the heavy bags that hung from the ceiling.

When they were teenagers, their daddy had turned the loft of his tinker barn into a gym of sorts for Cade and Shane. There were weights and two heavy bags and a couple of striking bags suspended from the ceiling. It was a place for his boys to blow off steam when they needed to, and both Shane and Cade still used it from time to time. From the sound of it, Cade needed it today.

Shane gave up calling to Cade and climbed the stairs.

Cade's face was blank as he threw punch after punch. Shane shut the music off but Cade didn't stop for a few minutes. When he finally did, his shirt was drenched through with sweat. He walked over to one wall and slumped down, resting his arms on raised knees and letting his head fall back to the wall.

Shane grabbed a bottle of water and put it by Cade's side and then sat against the wall, legs kicked out in front of him...and waited. There wasn't anything to do but wait. Cade may have been the more even-keeled of the brothers, but when he did blow, he blew hard, and Shane had learned you just had to wait for Cade to calm down before you talked to him. When Cade was ready, he'd tell Shane what happened.

Cade pulled the gloves from his hands and unpeeled the tape from around his knuckles before he finally spoke. "Mom got Laura to talk. They didn't know I was in the house. They don't know I heard the whole thing."

Shane didn't say anything. He and Cade had both known whatever story Laura had to tell would be a bad one. He didn't know if he really wanted to hear what Cade had overheard. He was pretty sure he didn't. Cade had seen and heard a lot of things because of the work he did with animals. For something to hit him this hard, it had to be bad.

"After her dad spent a lifetime treating her like crap, she meets this guy she thinks is Mr. Wonderful. He's all respectful and careful with her, and she thinks he's the one who's gonna save her from her father. She thinks he'll take her away and treat her right, that he'll cherish her. He didn't even try to get in her pants before the wedding. So even though her dad says he'll disown her if she marries Patrick, she does."

Cade swallowed down the rest of the water in two large

gulps. "You want to know why he never tried to touch her before they got married?"

Shane didn't answer. He didn't want to know. But he couldn't get the word "no" out. The pain etched on Cade's face had Shane frozen in place. He tried to swallow the painful lump in his throat and get something out. Anything that would stop what was coming, but he couldn't.

"You know why? Because he couldn't get it up if he wasn't hitting her. She didn't say it quite like that. I'm paraphrasing, but that's what it came down to. She was a virgin, and her husband raped her because that was the only way he could perform. So, she thought something was wrong with her. Can you imagine? She thought it was her fault. She said she didn't, but I could tell she did. Could hear the truth of it in her voice." Cade buried his head in his arms again and Shane wanted to do the same thing.

Laura was so tiny, so fragile looking. He couldn't imagine what it would do to her to have a grown man beating on her. Just picturing it made Shane feel as sick as Cade looked.

"You wanna know the first time he beat her so badly she couldn't leave the house for a week?" Cade asked.

"No," Shane managed to say this time, but Cade wasn't listening. He was staring at the wall like he was seeing the story he was telling, and he was too trapped by the power of it to see what was around him or hear Shane's voice.

"When her brother died. She wanted to go home to the funeral, but her husband had a business dinner she needed to attend. She had the nerve to ask him to postpone it so she could fly home for her brother's funeral. The irony was, she couldn't go to the dinner with him anyway. After the beating he gave her, she couldn't be seen in public for over a week, so she missed the flipping dinner anyway."

The brothers sat together without speaking for a long time. There was nothing to say. Shane couldn't imagine the fear Laura must have been living with every single day, the threat of having the person you thought you loved and could trust turn on you like that.

"I wish he wasn't dead," Cade said. Shane didn't have to ask why. He was thinking the same thing. If her husband wasn't dead, they could hunt him down and have the satisfaction of teaching him what it was like to be hit by someone so much stronger than yourself—to live in constant fear.

"Do you think his family knew? She said they lived right near them and saw his family every weekend. Do you think they knew?" Shane asked.

Cade nodded. "I don't see how they couldn't know."

They sat quietly brooding for a minute before Cade went on. "No wonder she ran. Even though he's dead, they can't get this baby. We can't let that family get this baby, Shane."

"I know. I've already started looking into the legalities of it. In a fair fight in court, they'd have very little chance of getting the baby, but it's likely she'll have to allow them visitation. Of course, with the Kensington family, who knows if the fight will be fair? I think when they put out the news that she was mentally unstable, they were already gearing up for a custody hearing. I think they'll try to show she's an unfit mother," Shane said.

"Then we need to help her make sure she's on her feet and providing for the baby when they find her. We need to make sure she has a shot at this," Cade said, pulling himself up and going to the fridge. He pulled out a beer and tossed it to Shane before pulling out one for himself and an icepack for his knuckles.

"Are you gonna tell her how you feel about her?" Shane asked, causing Cade to freeze, bottle halfway to his lips.

Cade eyed him and took the sip he'd postponed. "Heck no. Another man is the last thing she needs in her life right now."

"You're nothing like her father or her husband."

Cade didn't budge. "Doesn't matter. That's not what she wants or needs now. And, it's not what I need. I don't need another woman who—"

"Who what, might have to lean on you from time to time? Who might not always be strong on her own?"

Cade glared but didn't answer.

"Don't let Lacey do that to you. What she put on you isn't fair and you know it. It isn't your fault she tried to kill herself. She would have done that whether you broke up with her or not. She was sick and she needed help and you know it. Letting her put that on you is just you being a damn martyr," Shane said. He was tired of watching Cade's ex-girlfriend drag him down over and over again.

"I know what Lacey did wasn't my fault, but that doesn't mean I need to go out looking for it to happen again. I'm just saying, Laura isn't what I need right now, and I'm not what she needs right now."

Shane let it drop.

"Do you know what her brother's name was?" he asked instead.

Cade frowned. "James. I think her maiden name was Lawless. James Lawless. Why?"

Now it was Shane's turn to shrug. "I just thought we could see where he's buried. She might like to visit his grave or at least send flowers or something. If she didn't get to go to the funeral, maybe she's never been able to say good-bye to him. It's something we could do for her, that's all."

Cade threw Shane a hard look, but Shane put up his hands in defense. "Hey, I only have friendly feelings toward Laura; I swear. I'm not planning on stepping into your territory."

Cade growled. "She's not my territory. She's nobody's *territory*."

"Touchy, touchy," Shane said and headed down the stairs. Someone would have to run interference for Cade. If Mama took one look at Cade, she'd know something was up and Shane knew Cade wasn't going to want to talk about this.

"I'll tell Mama you're having dinner at your place tonight so you can watch the game. She'll buy that," Shane said over his shoulder. Cade lived above the horse barn but he ate most of his meals up at the house with Mama. "Get yourself together by tomorrow morning, though, or you'll have to come up with a better cover story yourself."

CHAPTER FIFTEEN

"So, Laura," Cade said as he packed hay into the slow feeders that leaned against one wall of the center aisle of the barn. Once filled, the feeders were hung in each stall to fend off boredom. The horses had to manipulate the feeder to work the hay out a bit at a time. "If you could grow things for a living, had start-up money and any resources you'd need, what would you grow?"

Laura didn't answer. She kept measuring grain into buckets and focused her eyes on the scoop of grain, not on Cade.

"Come on, tell me."

Laura stopped measuring and looked at Cade. "You really want to know?"

Laura was used to people not only assuming she wouldn't amount to anything, but also telling her that. It occurred to her that since she'd arrived on the ranch, no one had treated her that way. Instead, May, Cade, and Shane all acted as though she could easily be a contributing member of the ranch. When she asked what she could help with, they'd taught her how to help with the horses and thanked her for pitching in.

"I wouldn't have asked if I didn't want to know," Cade said.

Laura tried to sound nonchalant.

"I'd grow seeds."

"What? I thought you grew plants from seeds not the other way around. Well, I mean, I guess everyone knows that plants produce more seeds, but why would that be the focus instead of the plants themselves?" Cade asked.

"Because there aren't enough people breeding and growing organic seeds that are specifically bred to thrive in an organic environment. Most seeds are bred in conventional systems of gardening, and they perform best in those systems. When you take those seeds and plant them in an organic system, they don't do as well. It's sort of like taking a child who speaks one language and plopping her into a classroom where another language is taught. She would probably be able to do some of the things the class is doing just by following along, but she won't thrive," Laura said, then flushed as she realized he was watching her intently. She hadn't intended to say that much.

"How do you know that?" Cade asked.

Laura answered with a shrug. Cade continued to work quietly, as if he didn't care whether she answered or not.

Laura relented. "I read a lot about organic gardening. I would have loved to grow all our own vegetables, but Patrick thought that was...beneath us. He didn't mind my *little flower hobby*, but he drew the line at growing food."

"So, that's what you'd do if you could do anything? Breed seeds?" Cade asked with a grin.

Laura's heart shouldn't have skipped a beat when he grinned, but it did. She turned back to the grain buckets and tried to slow her suddenly much-too-fast breathing before she answered.

"Yeah. There's a science to it, but it's also creative and I'd be able to work with plants. My greenhouse was the only place I could be alone, be at peace."

"What would you need to get started?"

Laura busied herself with measuring grain. She didn't want to dream and fantasize about what couldn't be. She'd accepted a long time ago that there wasn't room for dreams in her life. She would soon have a baby to take care of. She needed a steady job, not a fantasy. And, she sure as heck didn't need to be dealing with the other feelings Cade's attention was raising.

"Laura, come on, humor me. It's fun to just dream sometimes," Cade insisted.

No, it's not. Dreaming leads to hope and hope lets you down every time. In the end, hope hurts like hell.

"Okay. A commercial-sized greenhouse. Just one at first, but eventually you'd need a lot more than one. And space for those greenhouses," Laura said.

"Texas has a lot of space. What else?" Cade asked. He crossed to the tack room and reached into the bin where he kept his bags of mints. He was back out in a second with carrots Laura had replaced the mints with in his hand.

"What's this, Laura?" he asked, eyes soft.

Laura smiled back at him sheepishly. He laughed and she stomped her foot at him. "Don't laugh. All those mints are bound to be bad for their teeth. I thought we could do carrots for a change."

Her heart raced as she waited for his reaction.

Cade snorted and shoved the fistful of carrots in his back pocket, leaving the green tops hanging out. "All right, but if we end up with a stampede on our hands tonight, or if all the horses rebel and refuse to come in for dinner, I'll know who to blame."

Laura couldn't tell if he was joking or not. "Will they really stampede?" she asked, her brow furrowed as she tried to read his face. Part of her was just relieved he hadn't yelled at her for hiding his mints. Another part of her was proud for having taken the initiative, for taking a risk.

Cade laughed some more and shook his head. "Don't worry. The worst they'll do is pout. But don't expect me to cover for you. I'm putting this change square on your shoulders when the horses ask where the mints are. I'll point the finger straight at you, Laura. Now, really, what else would you need to breed seeds?" Cade asked, bringing the conversation back around to her future plans before she could even take a minute to enjoy the satisfaction of voicing an opinion and making a change based on it.

Laura sighed and played along. "Pots and starter plants —organic starter plants or heirloom seeds—and soil and a few tools. Not much. A way to keep records of your crosses and backcrosses."

"A laptop." Cade nodded as though he were making a list in his head.

"It's just a dream, Cade. I'm not actually going to do it. I need to find a real job, a job that can keep clothes on my baby and food in our stomachs. A steady job with a reliable paycheck."

Cade just smiled at her as he began hoisting the feeders up onto the hooks in each of the stalls. "Never hurts to have a dream, Laura," he said.

But Laura knew better than that. It could hurt like hell if you weren't careful.

CHAPTER SIXTEEN

L aura was feeling settled on the ranch and actually wondered if she had overreacted. Maybe Patrick's family wasn't coming after her at all. She was still a little too frightened to get a job, and go through things like filling out tax forms, since that would identify her to anyone who might have the tools to seek her out that way. She was contributing to the ranch by helping Cade with the animals and helping May with meals and cleaning as much as she could.

Each day, Laura thought, *just one more day. I'll stay one more day.* But days turned into weeks, and she began to feel she could really stay. She could make this her home. Her child's home.

Laura loved the mouthwatering meals May was teaching her to make. She'd eaten in some of the finest restaurants in New York, Paris, Rome, and any number of other places she and Patrick had traveled to with his family or when they traveled with his business associates. She'd also cooked all her life for her father and brother, and later for Patrick.

Despite all that, never had she had such satisfying meals as those she cooked with May. They weren't necessarily gourmet. There just seemed to be something about them that made her feel at home. Maybe this was what people meant when they said something was "comfort food." Everything May served seemed to fit that description.

Putting her fork down on an empty plate, Laura enjoyed the last bite of her second helping of pot roast. It was so tender, knives hadn't been needed for anything more than to slather butter on thick slices of honey-wheat bread.

Shane and Cade were still packing away their third portions—extremely large portions, at that—but Laura really couldn't blame them. The meal really was incredible.

When Shane put his fork and knife down, he cleared his throat and glanced a little uneasily at Cade then at her, making Laura immediately tense. She had a feeling she wasn't going to like what was about to come out of Shane's mouth, and she could see May was getting ready to jump in and defend her if she needed it.

"Um, Laura, I uh...I've started researching what we'll need to do if the Kensingtons do find you. I figure you'll need to see a doctor sooner rather than later for the baby. Any doctor's visit should be confidential, but you just never know. They may have someone who can hack into records and track you." Shane glanced at Cade and then cut his gaze to May before hurrying on. "I think we need a plan in case they come after you.... Legally, I mean. They may try to sue for custody, Laura."

"Shane—" May began but Laura cut her off.

"No, he's right, May. Shane's right," she said as she placed her hand over May's. "I can't hide out forever. Some-day, I'll have to face them, and if they do try for custody, I'm going to need all the help I can get. Honestly, Shane, I'm touched you've started looking into this for me. I can't pay you right now, but I will. I'll pay you back on a monthly plan if I need to."

Shane shook his head. "You don't need to do that, Laura, but I will need some information from you." He looked over at his mother again, before meeting Laura's gaze. "And I need to ask you some questions that may be a little tough for you to answer."

Laura sat up straighter and raised her chin. She had wondered if Shane knew about the abuse. Cade seemed to have picked up on it, so she figured if Shane hadn't figured it out himself, Cade might have told him.

As she let the idea of all of them knowing sink in, she forced herself to accept it. She needed to get this out there if she was going to get past it. The story needed to be told to diffuse the power it held over her. "Ask away. What do you need?" She'd be damned if she would shrink away from what had to be done to keep her baby.

"Maybe we should go in the other room and talk?" Shane suggested, but she shook her head.

"You can ask me anything. I don't mind May and Cade hearing," Laura said. She'd already told May a lot of what her marriage had been like. In fact, she wasn't quite sure how May had gotten the stories to come out, but once they had, Laura felt like some kind of veil of shame, a veil of secrecy, had been lifted. It was okay to tell people what Patrick had done because it wasn't her fault. *She* hadn't been the one to do wrong. He had. The only thing she could fault herself with was staying and she was changing that now. She'd had a plan to run. When push came to shove, she'd been ready to protect her baby and she would hold her head high if for no other reason than that.

"It will help your case immensely if we can prove the

abuse, but also if we can prove that the rest of Patrick's family was aware of the abuse and didn't stop it or report it. Was the abuse ever documented or did you report it to anyone?" Shane asked.

Laura took a deep breath. She'd been ready for this day. She swallowed the last bit of panic at what she needed to do.

"Do you have a computer?" she asked.

Shane stood and crossed to the front door, picking up the bag that sat by his shoes. He withdrew a laptop and returned to the table, turning it on before placing it in front of Laura.

"About a year ago, even before I got pregnant, I knew I needed to leave him someday. I didn't know how I would do it, but it was clear I needed to or he'd eventually kill me. I wanted leverage if I ever left. He'd come after me. He wouldn't just let me walk away. But, I thought if I had proof of the abuse, I could get his mother to control him. She'd seen the bruises, but never helped. Never stepped in."

Laura took a deep breath and steadied herself. "I knew Martha's involvement would change if I had evidence I could take to the media. Reputation is everything to the Kensingtons. Keeping up appearances is more important than her son's pride. With embarrassing proof, his mother would have kept him from coming after me."

Laura paused for a minute and prepared herself for what she was about to do. She opened an Internet window and typed in an address. It felt eerie to do it. She'd actually never checked the email account since she opened it. She had set it up only to receive emails she sent to it. She hadn't given the address to anyone since the day she'd used a computer at the local library to create the account a year ago.

As she talked, Laura selected the tab at the top of the screen to organize the emails by sender, then scrolled through the junk mail to the section of emails she'd sent herself.

"I started saving little bits of money here and there. I'd wash and starch all of Patrick's shirts in the basement when he was at work. I put them on hangers I'd saved from the dry cleaners and put them with his suits when I brought them home. I could save twelve dollars a week that way. I clipped coupons and bought small things he wouldn't notice using our debit card, then returned them for cash."

Laura kept her eyes on the computer screen. She might be about to bare her soul to these people, but looking them in the eye was a bit more than she was ready for as she talked about the humiliation of saving a dollar here and there for her escape.

"I started an email account and took pictures on my phone, then deleted them as soon as I'd sent them to the account. By the time I found out I was pregnant, I had only saved three hundred dollars but I'd collected several months' worth of pictures. With the baby, I didn't have a choice. There wasn't any more time. I knew I had to leave right away. A week before Patrick died, I sold all of the jewelry in our safety deposit box and bought a new identity. I planned to leave when he was on a business trip. This email account was my safety net if he tracked me down."

Laura turned the computer toward Shane and stood up. The room was silent as she turned and walked out the back door. She couldn't watch. She knew what they'd see, but she didn't know what they'd think when they saw the pictures.

Would they wonder how she could have been such a fool to have trusted this man? Or that she was weak for not leaving right away? For staying for three years? Or pitiful because she hadn't stood up for herself?

Cade wasn't sure he was ready to see what Laura had just shared with them, but he almost laughed when he saw the email address she'd set up. *Proofhesabastard@gmail.com.*

Shane clicked on the first email, and any laughter dried up in Cade's throat. Shane clicked through email after email, picture after picture of black and purple bruises. The lawyer in Shane was meticulous. He carefully saved each photo in a file as he went, documenting the date and taking a screen shot of the email, as well.

Bruises littered every part of Laura's body. The imprint of hands clear as day on her skin where her husband had pinned her down, choked her. The evidence of punches hard enough to blacken large swatches of her tiny body. Black eyes and a split lip. A burn from...what? The hot pan she'd told May about? Something large enough to blister off a six or eight-inch area of skin on her back.

Cade felt sick. No one uttered a sound as he stood and followed Laura out the back door. She sat on the log bench he had carved out of a fallen tree for May. The bench set in a patch of wildflowers that grew ten yards from the back door; his mother's version of a flower garden. Cade made sure she could hear him coming up behind her, but she didn't move. Just stared out at the field of bluebonnets and yellow and pink Texas paintbrush in front of her.

Cade sat next to Laura and threaded his fingers through hers. Her hand was so tiny in his. The thought of her so small and defenseless and all alone facing that monster she'd married tore at his heart like nothing ever had. He'd seen Patrick Kensington on television—everyone had. He wasn't the largest man in the world, but he dwarfed Laura.

How had he ever thought she was weak? That she might be like Lacey? Laura was without a doubt the bravest woman he'd ever met. Her strength humbled him. She was as far from Lacey as any woman could ever be.

"I'm so proud of you, Laura," Cade said. He shook his head, unable to speak past the thickening in his throat for a few moments.

"If he had caught you collecting that evidence—God, Laura—I can't even imagine what he would have done to you. You were so brave to get yourself away from there."

Laura huffed out a sarcastic laugh. "But I didn't. Not really. I sometimes wonder if I would have had the guts to leave if he hadn't died. You know, it's horrible to say, but when the police were standing on my doorstep telling me Patrick had died..." Laura swiped at tears on her face. "I just felt relieved. All I could think was that I'd finally be free. My baby would be safe. I shouldn't have felt that when I heard that my baby would grow up without a father, but I did. I couldn't—I *can't*—feel anything more than relief that he's dead, and I hate that. I'm ashamed of it."

Cade squeezed her hand. "You don't ever have to feel ashamed of anything he made you do or feel. Of anything he did to you. Never feel ashamed of any of that, Laura. The man was a monster. But you, you're an amazing woman to have survived that. You're incredible."

CHAPTER SEVENTEEN

Morning chores finished, Laura and Cade walked up the path toward the main house together just in time to see a car driving up the long dirt drive. She tensed as the car drew closer, but Cade spoke quietly before she could decide which direction she should run.

"Go on up to the house, Laura. I'll see who it is."

Cade may have meant to set her at ease, but his instruction made her more anxious. It meant he didn't recognize the car. She had the sense the Bishops knew everyone around here, so a car Cade didn't recognize had a ball of knots twisting in her stomach.

May met Laura at the door and looked past her at the billowing dust surrounding the brown sedan that made its way up the drive.

"Cade doesn't recognize the car," Laura said.

"I don't either," May said shaking her head as she stepped aside to let Laura in. "But, that doesn't mean it's trouble. Could be one of our friends bought a new car."

Laura didn't believe May any more than May most

likely believed herself, but she smiled tightly and went along with it.

"You're right. It's probably nothing. Can I help you get lunch on the table?" she asked as they walked toward the back of the house to the kitchen. It took everything Laura had not to peel back the curtains and stare out the window as Cade greeted the stranger. But, if it was trouble, there was no better place for Laura to be than in the kitchen. She could slip out the back door and into the root cellar if Cade signaled that she needed to.

No sooner did she have the thought than Cade gave the all clear. "Laura, Mama, guess who's here?" he called out as they heard footsteps coming through the front door. The light tone of his voice told her there wasn't any threat. "Josh is here to visit with no set return date in sight."

Cade came through the kitchen door with a grin, and Dr. Joshua Samuels following along behind him. Laura's heart flipped over and relief flooded through her, leaving her weak. She hadn't realized how frightened she was until she knew she was safe. In that moment, she realized how complacent she'd become. Just how much she'd allowed herself to believe she could settle in and stay with the Bishops and that scared the daylights out of her.

"Joshua!" May's smile lit her whole face. Laura had a pang of longing when she looked at the two as they hugged. She didn't know what caused the feeling, really; as far as she knew, May and Josh were nothing more than old friends. But, there was an ease to the way they fell into one another's arms. Laura knew she'd never had that in her life and, suddenly, she acutely felt the lack of it.

She wanted that someday. More than she'd ever wanted anything.

Laura forced her eyes to pass over Cade as that last

thought passed through her head. She wiped her hands down the front of her skirt, and willed them to stop shaking.

Josh crossed to Laura and took her hands in his. "You made it."

His smile was genuine, though his face was filled with concern. Emotion flooded Laura but she swallowed it down. She knew she should probably embrace the feeling of being surrounded by people who cared, people who wanted her to be happy and safe. But, a minute ago, when Laura thought the Kensingtons had found her, she thought she might have to run, to leave the ranch. That was the worst thing she'd felt in a long time.

She'd let herself fall into this fairytale wonderland over the last few weeks, but she knew she couldn't risk getting used to the happiness and peace the ranch offered if that meant later she might lose it. She didn't want to have to wonder if at any moment someone could come to take away any happiness she found there.

May's arm came around Laura's shoulders. "She made it, and it's been wonderful having her here."

Panic set in. She'd let contentment and pleasure into her life, yet she knew it was too good to be true—she'd lose it sometime. The way things were now, she couldn't ever trust that the life she'd built here couldn't be taken away in an instant.

Laura steeled herself. "It's been wonderful being here. Even if it is only for a short time. I'll be moving on soon, though. I need to move to a bit bigger city to find a job, a place to live," she said, ducking her head.

She stepped out of May's embrace and crossed to carry a dish of potato salad and a plate of sandwiches to the table. Laura ignored the surprised looks crossing the faces of the others in the room and set out a pitcher of sweet tea to go with the large spread May had made for lunch. May always set out an enormous amount of food no matter how few people were expected, so having Josh at the table wouldn't be a burden at all.

Laura could feel the tension in the room as she buzzed around, finding ways to busy her hands until the moment passed. Except it didn't pass. She heard Cade murmur something to May and Josh, and was surprised when they left the room. She thought May would be the one to try to talk with her about staying longer, not Cade.

For the first time since she'd met him, Laura flinched when Cade spoke, even though she'd known it was coming.

His tone low, he spoke calmly, with the supportive look in his eyes she'd come to crave. "What's going on, Laura? Why are you talking about leaving again?"

Laura turned and faced him and let loose all the fear that welled up inside her, that ate at her, and brought self-doubt when she wanted to be strong. All the fear made her prepare to run when she wanted with all her heart to be able to stay. She turned that fear into anger and turned it on the man before her.

"What am I doing? You want to know what I'm doing? I'm not getting my hopes up, that's what I'm doing, Cade. I'm being realistic instead of living in some fantasy where I get to stay on a ranch where I feel safe, with people who care about me. With plenty of food and no one that wants to hit me." Laura's fists balled at her sides, her nails digging into flesh as she struggled to contain her emotions. But that battle was long ago lost. The emotions whipping through her took her last bit of control. "Where I don't have to worry about money or how to take care of my baby. Where I have love and support and…"

She shook her head as her eyes and nose burned with

the tears that were going to come no matter how hard she tried to fend them off.

"I can't do it, Cade. I won't hope for this. I won't let myself think I can have this, because it's going to hurt like hell when I lose it." Laura wrapped her arms around herself and ignored the tears she knew fell on her cheeks.

Cade just watched and waited though she was in the middle of a meltdown, in the middle of making a fool of herself. She hated losing it in front of him. Laura swiped angrily at the tears and turned toward the counter, searching for a distraction.

There must be some other chore she could do, something to focus on other than the man behind her who had never had to wonder when the earth would fall out from under his feet.

Cade wouldn't let her turn away though. He came around beside her and slowly reached a hand out to touch her with just one finger under her chin, gently pulling her eyes back to his.

"You don't have to leave, Laura. Ever. I promise you. You'll never have to leave here."

Cade wanted to reach out and hold Laura, to pull her in tight and wrap her up and protect her from all of her fears, from all of her memories, and all the things that chased her and wouldn't let her go. He wanted more than that. He wanted to kiss away those fears, to make love to her and make her forget—to erase all the hurt and pain she'd suffered.

But he knew, watching her now, she wasn't ready for any of that. She'd run like hell if he tried that. Even now, he saw a flash of anger in her eyes. The tears were gone.

"You're not the one who'd lose if that isn't true, Cade. What happens when they find me here and they try to take my baby? What if they win? Do you think a court isn't going to at least consider whether the baby wouldn't be better off with the Kensingtons instead of me? Patrick's family can give this baby everything. What do I have to offer? I don't even have a home of my own or a steady job. What will I do when the court says Martha Kensington will be a better mother to this baby than I will?"

Cade watched Laura try to collect herself, but it didn't seem to work. He had to curl his hands into fists by his sides to keep from reaching out for her. He couldn't deny that what she said had some merit, though he wanted to.

"You've had the comfort of knowing your whole life that you were loved and supported, and that you'll have that love and support no matter what. Well, I've never had that, and I'm not going to reach for it now. I *don't* want that. I *can't* want that," she said, raising her voice.

Cade didn't have time to answer. Laura walked out the back door and strode through the tall grass that led to Mama's wildflower garden.

Damn. He should have seen that coming. He should have been able to see that she'd been walking around pretending everything was okay, but she had never really let down her guard. She never really let herself be completely comfortable. She shouldn't have had to tell him that—he should have seen that himself.

Cade put his hand on the knob to follow her, but Josh's voice came from behind him.

"Let her be for now, Cade. She needs to figure out on her own that all of this isn't going away. And besides, she may be more right than you want to think," Josh said, looking back at May.

"What is that supposed to mean? Nobody's making her

leave." Cade said and wheeled around, turning on Josh with a lot more intensity than he intended.

"You might not make her leave, but that doesn't mean she won't have to run again. The Kensingtons are pushing hard to find her and the baby. They've had private detectives asking around at the hospital several times. I've been questioned three times by the PIs and once by the cops. The police took the security tapes from the day Laura left to try to see who she left with. I knew they might so I picked her up around the corner. All they saw was Laura walking away voluntarily and safely from the hospital, so the police aren't too keyed up about her disappearance...but the Kensingtons are. They're doing all they can to paint her as a mentally unstable woman who shouldn't be left to her own devices. I think they have very little use for Laura. Once they have that baby, I have a feeling they'll do all they can to get Laura out of the picture. Either fight for custody or have her committed to a mental institution—if they continue to push this mental-health angle. They're painting a really nasty picture for anyone who's willing to listen," Josh said.

"Do you think they suspect you were involved, Josh?" May asked.

Josh shook his head. "I don't think they did, but now that I've left they might. The staff will all tell them I take large chunks of time off each summer and it's not unusual for me to go away when I do, so they'll hopefully just chalk this up to a normal trip, or to me getting ready to retire. I was careful not to use any of my credit cards getting out here, and I actually took a few side trips along the way so they shouldn't be able to track me here."

"All right, sit and eat. You must be hungry by now. Laura will come back when she's ready," May said and moved to sit down at the table.

Cade looked at the table, but suddenly wasn't very hungry. He'd all but forgotten that Laura was on the run in the last week, and the brutal reminder didn't help his appetite.

"I'm not hungry, Mama. I've got some work to do out in the barn. I'll see you guys for dinner later," he said and left before his mother or Joshua could reply.

CHAPTER EIGHTEEN

Alec looked over at the doorway to Patrick's office as Justin entered. "Hey, I didn't expect you here. Something you need?" Alec asked, not letting his annoyance show.

The last thing he wanted to do was deal with Justin Kensington. There'd been no sign of Laura Kensington so far, and his search of all of the places he thought Patrick would have hidden the evidence he claimed he had was turning up nothing. He was tempted to believe Patrick had been bluffing, but he knew the man better than that. And, the risk was too great. He couldn't chance that information coming out.

Justin looked at him a bit strangely. "Yeah, I just thought I'd come clean out Patrick's office. Get his personal things, you know. I'm trying to take care of as many details as I can before I leave," Justin said.

Alec had Patrick's files stacked haphazardly on the desk. He looked down at them and back to the empty filing cabinet he'd been searching. "Yeah, I'm just getting these files out of here so my secretary can go through them and see what needs to be done with them. I'll get these out of your way so you can collect his personal things."

Alec began gathering the files. "Unless you'd rather I have my secretary collect his things and deliver them to your mom. You don't need to go through all of this now, Justin. We can take care of it."

Alec kept collecting files, striving for impassive indifference on his face as if he couldn't care less if Justin took Patrick's personal effects today or left them to be delivered later. But he'd be damned if he'd let Justin walk out of here with anything. Not until he was sure there was nothing that could incriminate him.

Before Justin could answer, Alec's day got a whole lot worse. His secretary announced Mark and Paul's arrival. He'd been expecting them for an update on the case and with Justin here, there was no way he could avoid letting Justin sit in on the update. If the private detectives were smart enough, they'd report that they'd found nothing and then give him an actual update later, but he doubted they'd pick up on that, or that they were smart enough.

And he was right. The two men walked in with a file folder in hand, and announced that they had news before they even saw that Justin was in the room with him.

No choice now.

"Great. Guys, you remember Patrick's brother, Justin," Alec said.

Both men nodded. "Good to see you again," said Mark, before opening the file and handing a sheet to Alec.

"We were able to get hold of Laura's phone and email info. She didn't send or receive very many emails from the account on her smartphone, but there was one email address she sent things to fairly frequently. She deleted the emails as soon as they were sent but the record of the address is still there," Mark said.

"What was the email address?" Justin asked.

Alec backed up and put his hand to his lower back. The familiar feel of the .22-caliber handgun he kept under his suit jacket there helped steady him. He couldn't actually shoot anyone in the office with his secretary and half a dozen other staff right outside the door, but if the detectives were about to reveal something that could get him in trouble, he would at least be able to get out of here without anyone stopping him. Alec's heart raced as he waited to see how this would play out.

"She was emailing *proofhesabastard@gmail.com*," Paul said.

Alec tightened his hand around the grip of his gun. He was backed into the corner of the office with Justin, Mark, and Paul all standing between him and the door. *Fuck.*

"We hacked into the account and realized Laura was emailing herself," Mark said.

What the hell? Was Laura the one who had the evidence the whole time? Maybe she told Patrick, not the other way around? He hadn't thought she was very smart, but maybe he'd underestimated her all this time. To be honest, he hadn't really paid much attention.

"Justin, we were planning to come see you after we talked to Alec. This, uh, this isn't going to be easy for you to see," Mark warned. The PI had an almost apologetic tone to his voice, and Alec realized it didn't sound as though the detectives had found anything that incriminated Alec in her account at all. In fact, their entire focus was on Justin right now.

"What are you talking about? What is it?" Justin asked.

"We didn't print anything. We thought it would be

better not to create any more of a trail than already exists. We need to log on to show you," Mark said as he gestured to the computer sitting on Patrick's desk.

Alec eased his hand off his gun and let his suit jacket fall back over it. He had already checked Patrick's computer. There wasn't any big file sitting on the desktop labeled in a way that screamed about Alec's guilt. "Yeah, go ahead. It's on." He waved a hand at the desk and moved between the men and the door as the others gathered around the computer.

A few seconds later, he watched Justin turn white and utter a curse he didn't think anyone of the Kensington caliber would know, much less say.

"Did you know about this, Alec? Did you know he was beating the—" Justin swallowed and looked at Alec. "Oh, God, did you know?" Justin asked, and Alec had to admit, the man looked truly stricken.

"What? What are you talking about?" Alec moved around the desk to look over Justin's shoulder and saw picture after picture of Laura Kensington, bruised and battered.

Alec looked across the desk to the two investigators. "Anything else to report?" They shook their heads. "You don't have a record of any of this? You didn't print or download it?" he asked.

"No, sir. Nothing."

"That'll be all for now. I'll call you to check in later," Alec said, dismissing the two men as Justin scrolled through more of the photos. When the door shut behind Mark and Paul, Alec spoke again.

"Justin, we need to get rid of this. We can't let this get out. It would destroy your mother, your brother's reputation," Alec said. He didn't want to take a chance that there was anything else buried in those emails that Justin might stumble on. "Don't torture yourself looking at those, Justin. We need to get rid of them and then keep looking for Laura. She must be terrified if this is why she's running."

"I need to talk to my mother," Justin said, still not taking his hand off the mouse as he flipped through the evidence of his brother's abuse.

"Go. I'll delete the account. What she went through was awful, but your brother is dead. Letting this get out can't help Laura now. All it will do is lead to speculation. People will want to know why he did this, if he was abused as a child, if your family knew he abused his wife. We need to make sure this doesn't get out."

Justin nodded numbly at Alec and then stood and left the room as though he moved on autopilot. How did this happen? How had Laura been living with such horrifying abuse without him having the slightest idea anything was wrong?

It happened because you were never here. You didn't care enough to stay.

Justin and Patrick had been two very different people. Patrick had somehow been able to handle the family and all its pressures and expectations. Then again, Justin thought with grim realization, maybe he hadn't been handling it so well after all. Not if what he was doing to his wife was any indication.

Justin hadn't ever handled it. As soon as he'd gotten hold of his trust fund at twenty-three, he was gone. He'd traveled, blown obscene amounts of cash, had very few ties with anyone, and had only visited his family when it was absolutely necessary. In fact, as he thought about it, he'd probably only seen Laura once or twice since the wedding.

But this level of abuse? He never would have guessed his brother capable of that.

Justin drove the twenty minutes to his mother's house with his mind spinning. His mother saw Patrick and Laura all the time. They only lived a few minutes away, and Patrick had been a mama's boy if ever there was one. How could Martha Kensington have missed all of this?

She couldn't have. There was no way she didn't know what was happening.

The thought made another wave of guilt wash through him. Guilt and disgust. His mother had turned her back on horrifying abuse. He was sure of it.

He let himself in and called for his mother as he started up the stairs. She'd been in her bedroom for days drinking enormous quantities of vodka. It was a pastime she'd perfected over the years. Justin knocked on the door but didn't wait for her to answer before opening it. She glared at him from the chair by the window. Apparently she didn't have anything to say in greeting.

"Did you know, Mom? Did you know Patrick was beating Laura?"

Justin's stomach dropped when his mother actually smirked at his question. "Stop being so melodramatic, Justin," she said with a dismissive wave of her hand. "She was a difficult woman to manage. He did the best he could with her."

Justin couldn't believe what he was hearing. *Manage?*

"What are you talking about, Mom? A man doesn't *manage* his wife. And what he was doing was not some small little incident here or there. I saw pictures, Mom. He was beating the crap out of her. He tortured her. You can't tell me you didn't see the evidence on her. You can't sit there and tell me you didn't know."

As Justin watched his mother, his mind raced, searching for some reason that might explain the blank indifference he saw on his mother's face. What could make a person turn their back on someone suffering the way Laura had? How could his mother simply turn away from another woman needing help?

"Laura has pictures. Dozens of pictures documenting the abuse. And, I'll tell you one thing. I've got just as much money and almost as much power as you do, and from now on, I plan to use it to make sure you never get near Laura and her baby. If you go after her in any way, I'll make sure those pictures get out. And, I'll make sure Laura has all the money and influence she needs to fight you. You won't win this fight, Mother. You won't get anywhere near that baby."

He didn't tell his mother he and Alec had just agreed to delete all of the evidence. She didn't need to know that. She just needed to believe the pictures existed and that he'd use them if he needed to. Besides, for all he knew, Laura had copies. She'd been smart enough and brave enough to arm herself with the evidence in the first place. She most likely had copies or printouts or something more as backup.

"How dare you threaten me?" she slurred. She tried to use the trick where she drew herself up straight and tall, adding another inch or two to her impressive height. The effect was diminished when she stumbled slightly and had to hold onto the wing chair she'd been sitting in to keep herself up.

And in that moment, a flash of thought pierced the anger and shock Justin was feeling. He searched his mind, looking through the memories of his time at home, when he hadn't been at boarding school or college or partying in Europe. His father had always been cold and distant with them, but had there been something more? Justin had spent most of his life away at school. Boarding school had begun for him at five years old, for Patrick at seven. He had vague flashes of memories of his mother with a bruise here and there, but nothing that had ever raised a red flag for him. Until now.

"Mom," he croaked out, raising a hand to reach toward her, to connect in some way. "Did Dad—"

She cut him off, hurling the heavy crystal class in her hand toward him barely missing his head.

"You always were useless. Running all over the place, sleeping with Lord knows who and partying your trust fund away. It should have been you that died, not my Patrick. It should have been you." Her face was twisted into an ugly rage of drunkenness and just plain hate.

She'd never been a very loving mother, but Justin hadn't ever imagined their relationship would come to this. He shook his head as he watched her sink back into her chair. There wasn't anything else he could say to her at this point. Right now, he needed to focus on Laura, to make sure she was safe. Then, he'd come back and try to sober his mother up, try to talk to her and find out if she needed help just as much as Laura had all these years.

But, first, he would make sure his mother didn't hurt Laura. Justin called Alec on his way over to a hotel and told him to double their efforts to find Laura and to send any bills for the detective work to him. He needed to make sure she was all right, and make sure she knew she could stop hiding and running. It was time someone in their family did the right thing for Laura Kensington.

CHAPTER NINETEEN

Laura tried to walk slowly so she wouldn't get to the barn too quickly, but it seemed like the trip was shorter than ever today. She knew she needed to apologize to Cade for yelling at him the way she had, but she didn't really want to have this conversation about it. She'd embarrassed herself enough as it was since she'd arrived at the ranch.

She'd seen Cade go down to the barn shortly after she had stormed out and she hadn't seen him leave in the last two hours, so he was likely still down there working with the horses or dogs.

Sure enough, as she rounded the corner, she saw him throwing hay bales into a stack along the center aisle of the barn. Light from the afternoon sun streamed in through the double doors to land on taut broad shoulders. The muscles in his back rippled under his shirt, drawing her gaze, but she blinked and tried to focus on the conversation they needed to have instead of the effect that watching him sometimes had on her body. Okay, the effect watching him *always* had on her body.

She knew he saw her because he stilled slightly before tossing the next bale onto the stack.

Laura waited, not sure how to start. She would have liked to get lost in him for a while instead of dealing with the awkwardness of her apology, but he stopped and wiped his brow with one arm, then stripped the leather gloves off his hands and looked at her.

"I'm sorry. I shouldn't have taken out my fear on you when you were only trying to make me feel better," Laura said, arms crossed over her chest. This was the first apology that felt true and real to her, and the first time she cared whether someone believed her apology was genuine.

In the past, apologies had been obligatory, either to avoid her father's wrath or to appease her husband and ward off further blows—to show the right amount of deference. She always knew a few more strokes would follow an apology for good measure, but it would eventually lead to peace. At least for a while.

But now, she cared what Cade felt and thought, only she couldn't read him. He merely looked at her. When she began to fidget, he held a hand out to her.

"Come here. I want to show you something," he said.

Laura laid her hand in his, so big and strong and protective. She tried to ignore the way that hand made her feel, the way his warm strength caused her body to thrum with electricity, but it was getting harder to push those feelings down. He tugged her out the back of the barn and around to one side where the Jeep she'd seen many times was parked.

"Shane was going to show you this later, but this is probably a better time," he said, opening the door and reaching into the glove box. Cade pulled out a set of keys and turned to sit on the seat of the car, long legs hanging over the edge. He pulled Laura into him so that she stood with each of her legs brushing the insides of his. They'd never stood this close—this intimately. He'd always kept his distance. But, now there was a closeness she hadn't dared to crave for more than three years. The heat from his legs brushing hers traveled, the warmth flooding her thighs and settling between her legs and making her chest tighten with anticipation, but he seemed unaware of the effect he had on her.

Cade held out the keys to her and pointed out the key to the Jeep. He looked her dead in the eye when he spoke, and she could see how much he meant the words he was saying. "This is always in here. If anything happens, if you even think someone is coming or you see anything suspicious, I want you to take the Jeep."

Laura opened her mouth to object, but he cut her off. "Take it, Laura. You need to have a way to get to safety if anything happens and I'm not here to protect you."

Her heart flinched at the thought that he would want to protect her. And, also at the thought that maybe he couldn't. She nodded at him.

Cade took out another key, looped on a chain, and held it up to her. It was a smaller key, brass with a number on the side. He drew a piece of paper out of the glove box.

"This is the key to a bus station locker. Shane had some business in Johnson City a few days ago. He went to the bus station there and put ten thousand dollars in cash in a locker. This locker," he said showing her the key and then the paper. "There are directions to the bus locker here. There are also times and meeting places."

Laura looked at the paper.

Noon, two days after you run: Baird Diner in Searcy, Arkansas.

Noon, four days after you run: Casey's Barbeque, Springfield, Tennessee.

The list went on specifying ten separate meeting locations spread out over the course of almost three weeks. Laura looked up at Cade, unable to speak.

"If you have to run and I can't go with you, this is where I'll meet you when it's safe. If I'm not there, it means it's not safe for me to come and get you yet, so you keep moving and get to the next meeting spot. If you get to the end, go back and start over at the top of the list. I'll be there for you as soon as it's safe. I promise you that, Laura. This is your running plan. This is what you do if you have to run."

Laura was stunned as Cade looped the chain with the bus locker key over her neck. The brush of his hands sent tingling sensations down her spine, but his words had a much stronger effect on her. They melted her heart. "There's a copy of the meeting times here in the car," Cade said as he put the paper back in the glove box and shut it. "And, there's a copy in the locker just in case you can't get to the Jeep and you have to run some other way. Just remember the bus station in Johnson City."

Laura couldn't say a word. She was flooded with more emotion than she'd felt since the day Patrick had died and she'd started running. But a different kind of emotion. One overwhelming and new to her.

"Remember when you said I've had a charmed life, never had to worry about not having love and support?" Cade asked.

"I..." Laura whispered, voice thick as she shook her head. She felt awful for what she'd said. For the unfairness of what she'd said to him because of her fears. He cut her off before she could say anything more.

"No, Laura, you were right. Other than losing my dad, you're right. And even that happened when I was an adult and better able to handle it than I would have as a child."

Cade laced both of his hands with Laura's and held them to his chest, pulling her body even closer to him. Their bodies aligned in an intimate way that she'd never shared with any man other than her husband. No, that wasn't right. She'd never had this type of intimacy, of closeness, with Patrick. Cade's eyes were heated and she couldn't look away. "So, believe in that. Believe in my charmed life. Believe that I always get whatever I want. Because I want you in my life, Laura. For as long as you want to stay. When you're too scared to believe in anything else, you can believe in that."

Laura's eyes were locked on Cade's face as her breaths went shallow. She couldn't pull her gaze away. His eyes burned with intensity and need. And it created something Laura didn't want to feel. *Hope.* The greatest of hopes.

And Laura had never been so scared in her life.

CHAPTER TWENTY

"What do you mean gone? When? Where?" Alec demanded.

The private detective at the other end of the phone didn't seem riled by Alec's temper at all, and that only pissed Alec off more. "He's gone on leave. Apparently, it's something he does every summer and it's not unusual for it to be for long stretches at a time. The hospital said Dr. Samuels is semi-retired and only practices part-time now. That's all I could get out of them. I think it's worth trying to track him down, though. The police have decided there's nothing to Laura's disappearance. They won't share the CCTV tapes from the hospital or the airport, but they said they have her on tape looking safe, not coerced, and quite well. They're saying she left of her own volition and there's nothing more they can do."

"That's crazy. She stands to inherit her husband's substantial estate and she's nowhere to be found? How could that possibly be of her own volition? I don't buy it. Find that doctor and see what he has to do with this. I've always thought it was a little odd for him to want to check a woman who was only a few months pregnant into the hospital just because her husband died. Why wouldn't he just send her home and have her family doctor check on her? Find out what the hell he had to do with Laura's disappearance and where that man went," Alec said and disconnected the call.

Dammit. What was Laura Kensington up to?

Alec hadn't gotten a good night's sleep since she'd gone missing. He stared out the window at the front lawn of Patrick and Laura's home. He'd kept the staff on so far, but he'd need to close up the home and send them packing soon. So far no one had questioned his presence there as he'd quietly searched through Patrick's things, but a cursory search wasn't cutting it. He needed to tear this place apart and no one could see him do that.

"Sir?"

"What!" Alec snapped at the gardener who stood just outside Patrick's home office door. The man blanched, but held his ground.

"I thought you should see this, sir. I didn't know who else to show. Mrs. Kensington has not been here at all since Miss Laura has gone missing, so I don't know if I should call her or..." the gardener said, letting the thought trail off.

"No, it's fine. What is it?" Alec put a calm mask on his face and waited with all the appearance of a patient man.

The squat tanned man in front of him produced a bag from behind his back. It was smeared with dirt, but he could see the contents plainly through the clear plastic. Cash. A lot of it.

Alec took the bag and dumped the contents on the desk, ignoring the dirt that marred the once-clean surface. A quick scan told Alec there was likely at least twenty thousand dollars in cash and what looked like a driver's license.

Alec picked up the rectangle of plastic and flipped it over. The picture was of Laura Kensington, but the name said Laura Keller, and the license was from the State of Rhode Island instead of Connecticut.

Alec stared at the license for a few seconds trying to figure out what the hell Laura Kensington—or whoever she was—was up to.

"Where did you find it?" he asked the man.

"Buried in one of the planters in the greenhouse. Miss Laura had always tended to the plants in the greenhouse herself, but since she's gone, I do it to make sure her beautiful plants don't die. I saw the bag sticking out from the dirt," the gardener mumbled, as if caught doing something he shouldn't have done.

"Have you told anyone else?" Alec asked.

"No. No, sir." He shook his head.

Alec opened his wallet and slipped the license into it, then grabbed a handful of the cash from the desk and tossed it to the gardener.

"This is yours. You never found the cash or the license. You've been saving money for a new car, a bit at a time if anyone asks where you got that amount of cash. Just make damn sure no one hears about this, you got it?"

The man nodded vigorously, holding the money as if he were afraid it might bite him. "Yes, sir. I understand."

"Oh, and one more thing. Stay out of the greenhouse from now on. I'll take care of searching the rest of the plants, but I don't want anyone else in there from now on."

Alec watched the man leave the room before lifting his phone. He'd have his lawyer take care of letting the staff go and closing up the house until Laura Kensington was found. They'd hire a caretaker to come once a week and check on things and a lawn service to keep up the property from time to time rather than the full staff that existed now. The lawyer could easily be fooled into thinking Alec was simply trying to help his partner's widow out by maintaining the home without keeping up the expense of a full staff. Alec sneered as he waited for his lawyer's secretary to answer the phone. Manipulating people had gotten all too easy to do. It almost took the fun out of things.

MARK ENTERED the hospital cafeteria and approached the table where he'd left his partner to call Alec. Paul handed him a cup of coffee. It wasn't half bad—which was good, considering they'd spent a lot of time here in the past few weeks.

"What'd he have to say?" Paul asked.

"Wants us to track down the doctor, make sure he doesn't have anything to do with this. I got a feeling the doctor's involved somehow, though," Mark said.

"Yeah, what makes you think that?" asked Paul, eyeing Mark over the rim of his cup.

Mark shrugged. "Just a gut feeling. You know what else I have a gut feeling about?"

Paul didn't answer but looked up, expectant.

"I have a feeling Alec wants more from Laura Kensington than just to find her and make sure she's okay, or to bring her back for Mrs. Kensington," Mark said. "I get the feeling Alec has something else riding on finding this lady."

"You think he'll hurt her when he finds her?" Paul asked.

"You and I both know Alec isn't the upstanding businessman everyone thinks he is. He's had his hands in some nasty dealings in his time. And, somehow, he always manages to come out smelling like daisies at the end of the day. He makes damn sure of it. I don't know why he wants her, but I don't think he has anything good planned for Laura Kensington."

Paul put his coffee cup down and looked Mark square in the eye. "Is that going to be a problem?"

Mark shrugged again, face bland—impassive. "Not for me. You?"

Paul shook his head. "Nope. Not for me. I just figure we need to be ready to cover our asses when things go pear-shaped on us. If we don't watch him, we're liable to get caught up in whatever Alec Hall has going on."

Mark nodded, then gestured across the room with his chin. "There's our favorite talkative nurse's aide."

Pollyanna—as the men called her—was making a beeline for them, a broad smile on her face. She was the type of woman who always seemed to be trolling for a man. The type of nurse's aide who gave those who worked hard a bad name. It appeared she usually went after doctors, trying to nail down one to keep for her very own, but lately the private detectives had monopolized a great deal of her attention. It seemed that PIs were exciting enough to draw her interest away from the docs—temporarily, at least. The men had been exploiting her as much as possible and planned to continue doing so now.

"Hello, boys." She sidled up to the table and gave them both a cheeky smile. "What brings my two favorite hunks here again?"

Without missing a beat, Paul launched into a lie. "We were supposed to be meeting Dr. Samuels to do some follow-up on the Laura Kensington case, but he must have forgotten our appointment. We were told he's gone on indefinite leave."

Mark affected a nonchalant look. "No biggie, really. It was just routine follow-up to close our files and now, instead of working the case, we can spend your coffee break with you." He graced her with his panty-melting smile, and she actually sighed and leaned in closer to him.

Good grief.

"He goes away all the time," she said conspiratorially. "Although, never without telling us when he'll be back. Some people are saying he's not coming back. That he's just using up his leave time and then he'll retire when it's over. He doesn't have any of his own patients anymore—he just covers for the other doctors and rotates around."

Paul grinned and glanced over at Mark. "Must be a nice life. We should take some time off, Mark. We ought to learn from our elders instead of working so danged much."

Mark grunted. "You might be right." He turned to face Pollyanna and tossed an arm around the back of her chair. "What does Doc Samuels do when he goes away? He have a fishing place or something like that?"

She took the bait easily, a sloppy smile on her face as she practically snuggled into his arm and purred like a damn cat.

Fish. Barrel. Bang.

"No, he goes to some ranch his friends own. Spends a few weeks there every summer. I bet that's where he is now," she said.

Paul guffawed. "Ranch! There aren't any ranches around here."

Pollyanna just smiled and shook her head at him, a small pout pushing out her polished lower lip. "Not here, silly. In Texas. Ever-something. Ever... Ever... Everwood, Evermont. I don't know. Ever-somewhere or other," she said with a flip of her hair.

"Well, we don't have any friends with a ranch so we'll need to find another way to spend our time off, won't we Mark?" Paul asked, a grin splitting his face as he eyed his partner. He knew if Laura Kensington was with the doctor, they'd find her soon.

CHAPTER TWENTY-ONE

L aura's stomach flipped and flopped as Cade drove her and May into town. She told herself it was only the trip into town that was making her nervous, but the way her leg pressed against Cade's when she and May piled into the bench seat of his truck probably had a little to do with it. Or a lot. She was all too aware of the physical contact that was stealing her breath and making her palms sweat.

But, the fact that she was headed for town also had her heart banging in her chest. It was the first time she had ventured away from the safety of the ranch since she'd arrived on the bus over a month ago. Even if people were willing to keep her presence here a secret because of their loyalty to May, showing her face in public was not easy.

Cade and May had convinced Laura to go to town for lunch, and she wanted to pick up a few things at the store while they were there. May squeezed Laura's hand and smiled at her.

"Guess I have to go out sometime, huh?" she asked, with a little laugh.

"It'll be fine. I promise," Cade said as he pulled his truck into one of the angled parking spaces in front of the Two Sisters' Diner. Cade lifted May's wheelchair out of the back of the truck and brought it around to May, before taking hold of Laura's hand and helping her down. For just a minute, Laura let herself savor the warm feel of his strong hand supporting her before forcing her thoughts back to reality. No point fantasizing about things she couldn't have and really didn't want anyway. She didn't want a man in her life right now. Didn't want to get used to relying on him to hold her up.

Yeah, you keep telling yourself that, girl.

"Can we run over to the convenience store before we eat? I want to pick up a few things while we're in town," Laura said, stepping away from Cade, trying to re-establish some sense of equilibrium. She now understood what people talked about when they said their heart was fluttering. Fluttering? Doing the samba. Trying to burst clear through her ribcage and out of her chest entirely. Same thing.

"Works for me. I have things I want to get, too," May said, and Cade fell into step behind the women as they made their way two doors down from the diner to the store that carried everything from groceries to pharmaceuticals and even a few automotive items. There was a bigger grocery store fifteen minutes outside of town in the opposite direction of the ranch, but this one had most of the necessities. Most people tried to limit the trip to the larger store to once a week.

A tinkling bell announced their arrival in the store, and a young woman with long hair the color of India ink and eyes almost as dark called out from a counter at the back of the store.

"Be right out!"

"It's all right, Jana. It's only May and Cade and Laura. We've just got a few things to pick up," May called back.

No sooner had Laura's name come out than the woman whisked herself to the front of the store, no doubt to get a good look at the infamous Laura Kensington.

May smiled and made the introductions. "Jana, this is Laura, Josh Samuel's niece. She's visiting with us for a while."

Jana made no attempt to hide her open perusal of Laura as she shook hands with her. "Is that what we're calling her?" she asked May. "Josh's niece? Well, sure, I'll go along with that. *Josh's niece*, it's a pleasure to meet you." The tall willowy woman smiled at Laura. Laura shook her hand with more than a little reservation.

"It's nice to meet you, too, Jana."

May put her hand on Laura's back and propelled her toward the other side of the store. "Well, we'll just get our things so we can get to lunch. Good to see you, Jana."

When they were a few aisles over, May turned her chair toward Cade and shoved the red plastic basket she'd picked up at the door into his hands. "You help Laura find what she needs while I keep Jana entertained. If we're not careful, she'll call half the town and then charge admission to watch Laura shop." May aimed her chair back toward Jana, who was, in fact, about to key a number into her phone.

Laura groaned but Cade looked expectantly at her, leaving her with little choice but to get the things she'd come for. She went to the vitamin aisle first and grabbed a bottle of prenatal vitamins before she headed to the cosmetics section. She didn't wear a lot of makeup, but she was used to wearing some, and since she'd left town with no notice, she had nothing more than a little lip gloss in her purse.

She'd have to find new colors and brands since she had been shopping for her makeup at the designer department stores for the last few years, but she didn't mind. A small smile played on her lips, and she chose a light rose shade that she thought would go well with her new darker hair color. It would be fun trying to find the right look for the new Laura.

"Why do you need that? You're beautiful. You shouldn't cover your face with that stuff."

Cade's words were so reminiscent of the way Patrick would "suggest" she not cut her hair short, or "encourage" her to wear lighter shades of lipstick that were more becoming a woman of her stature in the community, that Laura hurriedly replaced the makeup on the shelf before she realized what she was doing. Both of them recognized what had happened, and an uncomfortable silence froze the air between them.

"Laura, I'm so sorry. I didn't mean it that way. I'd never try to tell you what to do. I just meant that you look beautiful without makeup."

Laura looked up at Cade, torn between wanting to find out how beautiful he thought she was, and wanting to punch him in the gut for making her feel like she couldn't buy makeup if she wanted to. Before she could decide, Cade started scooping makeup off the shelf and into the basket.

"You should definitely get some makeup. It'll look great on you. Here," he held up a shade of fuchsia lipstick Laura wouldn't wear in a million years. "This will look perfect. We'll get this one and a few others."

Laura couldn't help herself. Laughter started to bubble out of her, and she couldn't stop once she started. The picture of Cade shoving as much makeup as he could into the basket on his arm was something she'd never forget. He looked mortified, so completely repentant, but also just so darn silly with all that makeup in his hands.

Cade stopped and stared as more laughter poured forth. Then a slow smile formed on his lips and Laura's eyes locked onto those lips. The laughter dried up and her throat was suddenly tight.

"Well you two sure are having fun," came Jana's amused voice and Laura left the spell she'd fallen under behind, shaking it off as she turned to look at May and Jana.

"I think I'm all set here, May," she said as she put most of the makeup Cade had pulled off the shelf back. Leaving a blush, mascara, and two lipsticks in the basket, she walked to the counter to pay for her things.

Cade watched Laura as she wheeled Mama toward the diner. He stayed just two steps behind thinking about what had happened in the store.

What had happened?

One minute he'd felt like the world's biggest louse for trying to tell Laura she shouldn't wear makeup. He was sure her husband had probably been controlling, and the look on her face had confirmed that. But then she'd been laughing, happier than he'd ever seen her and that laughter cut through him as much as her pain had. It drew him like nothing ever had. He wanted to hear that over and over from her, to make her laugh every day. To make her laugh enough that she'd forget everything she'd been through.

Cade caught up to Laura and May at the door to the diner and pulled it open for them. Naturally, the low din of conversation came to an immediate and complete stop as soon as the trio entered.

Cade cleared his throat and spoke to the room at large.

"Laura, Evers. People of Evers, this is Laura, Josh Samuel's niece."

That brought a roar of laughter from the crowded tables of the diner and an end to the awkward moment, just as Cade had hoped it would. He helped May out of her chair and locked the brake, leaving it in the corner by the entrance. He let May lean on his arm as they walked toward a booth at the far left of the long room. It was opposite the counter that fronted the grill manned by Tina, one of the Caswell sisters. The other Caswell sister, Gina, approached the booth with coffee pot in hand and a broad smile on her face.

"Mornin' Laura—Josh Samuel's niece," she said with a wink. "It's good to finally see you out and about. We thought maybe we'd have to drive out to the ranch if we ever wanted to meet you, but that would mean closing the diner down for the afternoon, and Tina said that wouldn't sit well with folks."

"Tina?" Laura asked, eyes flicking to Cade's face.

"Laura, this is Gina Caswell. Her sister, *Tina*, is behind the grill back there," Cade said, nodding to the back where Tina's bright red hair—so clearly from a bottle and not a gift of genetics—poked up.

"I like the hair, Laura," the woman called out over the counter. "Much better than that washed-out blond in all your pictures. You should keep it this way."

Laura gasped and looked at Cade, who just laughed, along with all the other customers in the diner.

"Honey, you'll get used to it," Gina said. "We've all seen every picture out of your wedding album by now, the way the news is going on and on about you. This town is bad enough with most normal people, always all up in your business. But, you? *Hmmpf.* You don't have any secrets anymore, sweetie."

Cade could see the subtle hint of panic on Laura's face and he guessed her mind had flashed to all of the things she'd never want a stranger to know. All of the things she shared with May, but probably would be embarrassed for anyone other than May to know. She'd certainly be upset to know he overheard it all and the thought that the whole town might someday know was bound to cause her to want to flee. Cade pulled her hand over toward him and rubbed his thumb over her palm. He'd meant to soothe her, but damn, if he didn't have to take a minute to tell his body to sit the hell down. His response to the small touch shouldn't have been so strong.

"It's okay, Laura. She didn't mean anything by it," he murmured quietly, so Gina wouldn't hear. May pushed closer to Laura in the seat, as if supporting her.

Gina gave Laura a sideways look. "I'll give you guys a minute," she said before heading to the kitchen. When she came back out a few minutes later, the trio ordered their lunch and the restaurant's din of conversation resumed.

Temporarily, at least. Two minutes after their food arrived, the peace was interrupted again when the door opened and a man wearing a tan uniform entered. All eyes swung to Laura but May's arm was immediately around her.

"It's an election year, sheriff," an older gentleman called out from across the room. "Hate to see you make any mistakes in handling a delicate situation."

The sheriff's eye crinkled up in laughter and he raised a hand in greeting. "Thanks for the reminder, Holland. I'll be sure to keep that in mind," he called out, his tone wry.

"He's a friend, Laura," Cade said under his breath as

Sheriff John Davies approached the table. The sheriff gestured to the seat next to Cade. May nodded and he sat.

"Friend or not, Cade, I was hoping I wouldn't run into you guys. Now that I've seen Mrs. Kensington, I can't ignore the fact that the whole country—with the exception of everyone in this county apparently—is looking for her." He spoke quietly, and Cade guessed he didn't want the whole diner listening in. He didn't want that either, but the other diners appeared to be listening intently anyway.

"John," Cade started, his voice a low growl.

"Cade," May interrupted, "John has a job to do. Let's let him do it and see where this goes. Laura, Sheriff John Davies. John, this is Laura, but she's more comfortable being called Josh's niece for now if you don't mind," May said with an indulgent smile.

Cade remained tensely coiled next to John, watching every move his friend made. He remained silent as Laura spoke. "It's nice to meet you, Sheriff."

John smiled at her. "Call me John. When all of this is over, Cade will remember we're friends and any friend of Cade's is a friend of mine." Cade's only response was a snort.

When Laura nodded, he continued. "So, it seems the police in Connecticut are pretty interested in your whereabouts." John took a French fry off Cade's plate and popped it in his mouth. "And your safety, in particular."

Laura nodded again. "I know."

"Did you come to Texas voluntarily, Laura?" John asked, ignoring Cade's scowl as he continued to eat his friend's lunch.

"Yes, I did."

"And you're staying here voluntarily? No one's keeping

you here against your will?" Cade rolled his eyes while May laughed.

"Yes. I'm here voluntarily."

"I understand congratulations are in order," John said, taking a sip of Cade's sweet tea.

"Jeez, John!" Cade said, but May shot him a glare.

"Watch your language, Caden Samuel Bishop," May said.

"When my sister was pregnant, she was plagued with morning sickness something awful. Couldn't keep anything down for months. You look like you're handling food better than she was," John said, nodding at Laura's plate of meatloaf, mashed potatoes, and glazed carrots.

Laura loosened up a bit. "It was really bad up until two weeks ago. That, and the exhaustion. I'm feeling better now."

The answer seemed to satisfy John, who had moved on to Cade's burger, taking half for himself despite Cade's raised brow. Cade relaxed enough to pick up the other half and begin to eat, but he wondered what John planned to do now that he seemed to be finished asking questions. The whole diner seemed to be waiting for his verdict.

John wiped his mouth on a napkin and stood. "Well, it seems to me you're of sound mind, despite the reports on the news, Laura. You don't seem to be any danger to yourself or your baby, and you don't seem to be here against your will. I have to report that I spoke with you, but as far as I'm concerned," John raised one hand toward Cade, who was halfway out of his seat at the mention of reporting Laura's presence in town. "I don't see any reason I have to give them any more information than that. I pulled you over. After speaking with you, it was clear you were of sound mind and body and no harm to yourself or others. You were simply a widow passing through on her way out of town. Last I saw, you were headed toward Dallas to catch a flight. Heck if I know where you were going after that."

A woman with two teenagers at her table spoke up. "She stayed a few days at my bed and breakfast, sheriff. Lovely woman, that Laura Kensington. I think she was on her way to New York City to visit a friend."

"I heard it was California. Said she wanted to see the west coast," Holland spoke up again. Others murmured rumored sightings and hints of a trip to Arkansas.

Laura and May smiled.

"Well then, Laura. It was very nice to meet you. I'll see you when Cade decides he's forgiven me, and I'm invited back out to the ranch for Sunday dinner sometime."

Over Cade's grumbling, May chimed in. "Anytime, John. You're welcome anytime you want to join us."

"Come on, John. I'll walk you out. I want to run over to Jansen's and put in a special order for a few things at the ranch," Cade said and turned to Laura and May. "I'll meet you back here in fifteen minutes."

"What are you getting for the ranch, Cade?" May asked.

"A greenhouse. A big, giant, commercial-sized greenhouse," he said grinning and shooting a wink to a shocked-silent Laura.

CHAPTER TWENTY-TWO

Mark shoved his chair back from his desk in the cramped, single-room office. He looked up at Paul, who sat at the desk across from him.

"Well, so far there's Everman, Evadale, Everwood, and Evers," he said, tossing his pen down on the desk.

Paul shook his head. "That's a lot of ground to cover when we don't even know if the doctor knows where Laura is. Maybe we should check with Alec to see if he wants to spend that kind of money to hunt down a lead that's thin, at best."

Mark raised his hands. "Not it. I called him with the last bad news. Your turn, pal."

Paul uttered a curse but picked up the phone to make the call. Neither of them liked dealing with Alec Hall. Dealing with that man was more dangerous than sleeping with a venomous snake in your bed, but he paid good money. A lot of it.

While Paul talked to Alec, Mark began to narrow down the search. He looked up each town, trying to decide if any could be ruled out. Two of the towns didn't have a website, and the others' sites didn't give any clue as to whether it would be the kind of area that would have a ranch in or near it. All of them looked to be far enough away from the larger cities that a ranch was a possibility. So far, he wasn't having any luck narrowing down their choices.

Paul put his phone down. "Wants us to check them all out. Every one of them."

Mark groaned without taking his eyes off his computer screen. He opened a new window and began to buy plane tickets to Austin, Texas.

"I'll get tickets. You book a rental car. We'll fly into Austin and work our way across the state. Let's start with Everman and Everwood. Those seem closest to what Pollyanna remembered. Evadale is Eva not Ever, but she could have gotten mixed up and if it was Evers, it seems like she would have remembered that and not thought it was Ever-something."

Paul's raised eyebrows said he didn't believe Pollyanna was capable of that level of thought any more than Mark did.

CADE WATCHED Laura laugh with his friends, and couldn't believe how much she'd changed since she'd come to the ranch. As they sat at a corner table at Pies and Pints, he thought about how much more relaxed she'd been since the day they went into town. It seemed as though a wall had come tumbling down after Laura saw the support the town gave her. Even Cade had found himself forgetting there was anything unusual about her situation.

Well, except for the fact that she was drinking club soda because of the baby she was carrying when everyone else was sharing a pitcher of beer over their pizza. No one seemed to mind. Alice and Stacey, two women who hung out in the group of friends that Cade and Shane generally saw a few weekends a month, had asked Laura a bit about her plans for the baby when they first arrived. Baby names and plans for a nursery and so on.

Laura had ducked out of those questions tactfully. Cade knew she still wasn't ready to commit to staying, much less painting the room May kept pushing on her as the nursery. But, he thought she was getting closer. She'd visited the clinic and seen the midwife for a checkup after being assured she wouldn't have to show ID to anyone, or use her real name if she preferred not to have it recorded.

Watching her now, Laura was animated and happier looking than he'd ever seen her as she listened to Stacey's boyfriend, Grant, tell a story about Cade and Shane's propensity for cow tipping when they were younger. She turned wide eyes on him.

"*You* went cow tipping? I can't believe you would do that!"

Cade winced. "We were young and stupid and completely convinced we could get away with it. When Dad found out, he sent us over to that farm to muck stalls and clean water troughs and do all the dirtiest chores they could think of for a month. Needless to say, it's not something I'd do nowadays. Scares the poor cows half to death," he finished with a cringe.

"Doesn't stop teenagers from doing it now any more than when you did it back then," came John Davies' voice behind him.

Cade swiveled in the booth to see his friend watching him and Laura warily. "Am I forgiven for grilling Laura yet, or do I need to find somewhere else to sit?"

Laura stuck her tongue out at Cade before she answered for him, and Cade was torn between being relieved to see her so playful, and being distracted by thoughts of what that tongue could do. He shifted in his seat and tried to banish the images from his mind, but it was no use. Those images were seared in. *Hell.*

Cade couldn't help but feel a twinge of jealousy as Laura turned a smile toward John. "You're absolutely forgiven for doing your job, sheriff. I know you couldn't just pretend you didn't see me."

Now Cade felt a lot more than a twinge. Why was she smiling at him so sweetly? And when had she become so danged confident? Cade knew women considered John attractive. John had more than enough single women—and even some married ones—throwing themselves at him. When he first moved to town years ago, the police station had received a fair number of calls at the station that weren't really emergencies. They were thinly veiled attempts single women made to get his attention—or their mothers were trying to set them up. That had slowed down some, but it still happened often enough to entertain everyone other than John. Until now, Cade had taunted his friend about it whenever it happened.

The thought of Laura smiling at John wasn't even remotely entertaining to Cade, and that, in and of itself, ticked him off. He had to find a way to get the feelings he had for Laura out of his head. She was trying to rebuild her life, and for the first time ever, she was trying to do that without the complication of adding a man to the mix. He'd heard her tell his mother she needed to learn to stand on her own two feet instead of leaning on a man.

And he needed her to do the same thing. Well, not exactly, but he needed to find a woman who didn't need to lean on him. Who could stand on her own two feet, and who wouldn't tie her entire existence to him as if she couldn't have her own identity without him.

"Cade, you still with us?" John asked.

"Huh? Yeah, just...yeah." Looking around the table it was clear he had missed something.

"I was just telling Laura the local officer I talked to in Connecticut was satisfied when I told him I saw her, and she seemed healthy, happy, and down here voluntarily." Laura was beaming at him from across the table. "They didn't seem at all concerned that anything had happened. The detective I spoke with said the family has been pressuring them and trying to get the police to begin a national manhunt for her, but when they looked at video footage from the hospital and the airport, there was no sign of foul play, and no sign that Laura was in any danger or was any danger to her baby. They've been telling the family for weeks now there's no active case, and there's nothing more they can do if Laura doesn't want to come home."

"You mean go back there. Not *home*. That's not home. Laura's home now," Cade said, smiling at her.

CHAPTER TWENTY-THREE

L aura nodded and smiled at Cade and the others but it felt stiff. *Home.*

Could it really be that simple? Could she really just stay with the Bishops? Take their charity and their kindness and live off them? Raise her baby there? But for how long? Surely she couldn't just live there forever?

Even if the police weren't coming for her, that didn't mean the Kensingtons would just give up trying to get custody of her baby once it was born. Laura needed to talk to Shane and see what he'd discovered. He had told her he was looking into the case law in this area, and he was sure a grandmother wouldn't have a very strong case for taking a baby from its mother without some very strong extenuating circumstances, but Laura wanted to be sure. She wanted to know she was finally free.

"Well, I have to get back out there. I'm on patrol for another two hours," John said as he stood and took another slice of pizza for the road.

"We should get going too," Stacey and Grant said and Alice nodded and stood with them.

"It was so great to finally get to spend some time with you, Laura. Maybe we can all go out again soon?" Alice asked Laura.

Laura smiled and nodded. Maybe she really could have this. A life filled with real friends and people who cared about her. A place she could truly call home. And...

Laura's eyes met Cade's and she knew she must be blushing. Maybe, someday, she could have someone who would love her and treat her as if she were a person who mattered, not a possession to be owned and conquered. Someday.

CADE STARTED to drive past the barn, but Laura stopped him.

"I'll help you with the nighttime bed check if you want," she said. That's what May always called the last barn check of the night. The one where you turned off all the lights, made sure the stall doors were shut properly, and checked to be sure none of the animals were having nightmares—or so May told her.

Cade glanced her way and slowed the truck, steering it toward the barn instead of the house. "Thanks."

A motion sensor kicked on the outside light as soon as the truck pulled up to the double barn doors. Cade jogged around to help Laura down and then pushed open one of the doors, flicking on the center aisle lights. It didn't take either of them long to see that Red was worked up over something. She was panting and pacing up and down the aisle but ran to Laura the minute she entered the barn.

"What do you think it is?" Laura asked Cade as she knelt to rub Red's ears.

He went to where Red had been pacing and looked over the top of the half door that led to the tack room. He grinned and waved Laura over. Red circled Laura's legs, nearly taking her down as she joined Cade to peek over the door.

"Oh my gosh, is she in labor?" The mother cat who had taken up residency in the tack room was panting and circling, pawing at her bedding. She circled a few more times before lying down, but she continued to pant.

"Looks like it," Cade said. "Want to wait up and see some kittens?"

They stood looking over the door together and when Laura turned to Cade and nodded, she realized how close their faces were. Close enough for her to smell the scent of peppermint from the gum he'd been chewing on the drive home. Close enough to see the stubble on his chin that had grown since that morning's shave. She wanted to reach out to touch it, to brush the tips of her fingers across it and see if it tickled her skin. She was close enough to wonder what it would be like to have those lips pressed to hers, to feel his arms come around her as he pulled her against his body and kissed the breath from her chest.

"Yes," Laura said huskily. She cleared her throat. "Yes, let's wait for kittens. Will she let us in there with her?"

Cade watched Laura for a beat longer, and the air swirled thickly between them. He took a step back, breaking the spell, then slid the latch on the door.

"I think so. I've been tossing chicken to her whenever I walk by the room or have to come in for something. She doesn't hiss at me anymore. She's probably a little too distracted by the labor right now to care anyway," he said as he took Laura's hand and pulled her into the room with him.

Red came and lay down on the floor near the door, getting no closer to the cat than she had to. It seemed as though she didn't really know what to make of the situation, but she sure wasn't going to leave her people in here without standing guard over them.

"I'll be right back. I'm gonna grab some drinks for us so we can settle in for a while," Cade said and he slipped out of the room. Laura watched the cat pant and knelt down in front of her. The cat turned wide eyes to her as though she didn't know if she should trust Laura so close to her.

Laura couldn't help but think how much this must hurt. "When the pain gets to be too much, baby, just go somewhere in your head. Go to your favorite place and leave all the pain behind. Just let it all go."

Laura heard the door hinges behind her and Cade stepped back in.

He put a pile of blankets next to the wall, then set two bottles of water on the floor and sat down. He pulled Laura down next to him. Her heart skipped a beat at the contact, at the way his hand swallowed hers. But, when he arranged her so that she leaned against his chest, her back to his front, and put those strong arms around her, wrapping her tight, she thought she'd burst from the utter happiness that shot through her.

Laura leaned back, soaked in the contact, and let herself get lost in the feel of Cade holding her tight. He'd probably done this with dozens of women and thought nothing of it, but this was special to Laura. It was incredible. Two weeks or a month ago, maybe even a day ago, she probably wouldn't have let herself relax, let herself enjoy the feel of just being with a man like this.

Now, Laura wanted to grab on to all she could while she was here. Sometime in the last few days, the last few hours, she'd decided if she had to leave here someday, she would damn well take some good memories with her.

She would find out what it was like to laugh with people, to have friends, to have what almost felt like a family, and to be with a man who could make her feel this wanted, this safe, this special. It felt better than anything Laura had ever known.

"Here comes the first one," Cade whispered in her ear. He probably hadn't intended it, but the feeling of his hot breath brushing her ear, her neck, sent shivers through her. Very good shivers she wanted to experience again. Laura closed her eyes for a brief moment and let the heat rushing through her body warm her.

"What do we do?" Laura asked. She thought of all the people that were typically in attendance at a birth for a human. A doctor, a couple of nurses, family. Surely they should be doing something for the cat and her kittens.

"Nothing," Cade said, a bit of a laugh on his breath. "Nature takes care of everything. As soon as the kittens come out, mom licks them clean, that stimulates breathing, and they nurse. It's that simple. Unless something goes wrong, we just sit back and watch."

They were quiet for a few minutes before Cade broke the silence.

"Where did you go when it hurt too much, when the pain got to be too great?"

Clearly, he'd heard her conversation with the cat moments ago. Laura didn't answer for a minute. Remembering where she went carried another type of pain with it. The pain her brother's loss always brought when she remembered he was gone.

"When we were little, my brother and I would go to this abandoned house down the street from us. Teenagers used to hang out there at night and party, but during the day, we were the only ones there. He'd make up silly games for us to play and we'd run through the rooms and just...just be away, you know. Away from Dad."

"You miss your brother?" Cade asked the obvious question, but she knew he genuinely wanted to know the answer.

Laura nodded. "He was usually able to convince me that I was special, that someday, I'd be loved. He would tell me about my mom; how beautiful she was. How much she loved me even though she was gone."

"How did she die?"

"In a convenience store robbery when I was just a baby." The answer came out hollow to her ears. She didn't know how she missed a woman she couldn't really remember, but she did. Her mother had been shot over a piddly amount of money and a six pack of beer some junkie wanted, but couldn't pay for.

They sat quietly for a long time, waiting for the kittens to come.

"What are you thinking?" Cade asked in a bit of a whisper, as though he wondered if he was breaking into her thoughts when she'd rather he didn't.

"I'm afraid to do this all alone. She looks like she's ready for the birth somehow," Laura said, nodding at the mother cat. "I'm completely unprepared. I don't have any idea how to be a mom, or what to do when I go into labor or what I need when the baby comes home, or anything. I've never been so completely unprepared for anything in my life. And the worst part is, nothing has ever been so important in my life before. I'm about to take the most important test I'll ever take with no textbook or teacher or anything."

"You don't have to be alone. It's more than okay to just

stay here and let Mama help you. I know you think that makes you weak, relying on other people, but it doesn't. Being brave enough to stick around, to make connections and ties, to gamble on people again after all you've been through—and considering all the people who've let you down—that takes guts."

Laura didn't say anything, but she hoped Cade was right, because she wanted to stay more than anything now. And, she wanted to believe that it would be all right for her to do that.

Cade watched Laura process his words and realized how much he believed what he'd said. Laura was strong. He'd been thinking she was too much like Lacey, that she'd need him to prop her up too much. But, she didn't. In fact, it was just the opposite with Laura. He had to fight to convince her to let him help, to let him support her and care for her.

Cade felt Laura lean back into him further. Was she relaxing into the possibility of staying on the ranch? It felt as though she were letting herself believe, if only for just a minute, that she could stay. He hoped she was. As he held her close, he realized he had no desire to let her go any time soon. Holding her felt better than anything he'd felt in a long time...and, maybe ever. He held his breath, hoping she'd let him hold her for a while longer. Just a little while.

Laura gasped as the first kitten arrived, covered in a dark sack of wet, gooey mess. "Wow, it sure isn't pretty, is it?" she asked and laughed.

Cade laughed with her. "Nope, not pretty at all, but I never get tired of it. We've had kittens born here, puppies, foals, even a donkey gave birth here once. And, back when we ran the ranch, we had cattle calving all the time. It never gets old. Even watching chicks hatch is amazing."

They watched as the mother cat licked the kitten clean. Within minutes, she looked a little more like a kitten and less like a blob.

"How long before the next one?" Laura asked, turning her head slightly to look at Cade.

Cade couldn't keep his eyes off her mouth, so close to his. A few inches and he could touch his lips to hers, test to see if she'd really let him. See if her mouth was as soft as it looked. He wasn't entirely sure he was breathing any longer. Or entirely sure if he cared. Who needed oxygen, anyway?

"Could be minutes, could be hours. We won't know how many she'll have either. Probably two or three, but she could have more. It's always a mystery with strays."

Laura turned back around.

Damn.

The kitten nursed hungrily, its eyes still closed, ears scrunched up like they were still closed off, as well. Cade watched Laura's face and could see the wonder in her eyes. He knew how she felt.

They watched as two more kittens appeared, to be cleaned by the mama cat and begin nursing.

"It's hard to tell with them still wet, but we have at least one orange kitten, one calico, and then either a black or gray kitten. It's probably time for us to name the mama and we'll have to find names for all of the kittens. At least temporary names until we adopt them out," Cade said.

"When will they go to new homes?" Laura asked, turning her head again, putting those eyes, that mouth into tempting territory again.

Cade swallowed and fought the urge to press his lips to hers. "Six weeks or so."

Laura turned around again and Cade wanted to curse.

He liked it better when she was twisted to face him, even though he had to fight not to pull her closer and crush her mouth with his.

"Another baby," Laura cried and Cade pulled his eyes from her to watch one more baby deliver. This one was larger than the others, but Cade saw no movement as the mother cat licked at the sack, tearing it open. He watched a minute longer, but saw no results from the mama cat's efforts to stir her kitten.

"Shoot," Cade pushed Laura up and hauled himself to his feet, grabbing a towel from one of the shelves above them.

"What's wrong?" Laura asked as Cade lifted the limp kitten.

"Hopefully just a little liquid in its airway. If I can clear it, it should be fine. If it's anything more than that, there's not much I can do."

Cade held the kitten between his large hands and turned it gently but firmly upside down. Then he rubbed its sides with the towel, watching for any sign of breathing. He'd done this before, sometimes with good results, and other times with no results at all. But, he'd never held his breath quite as tensely, hoping for the best result.

He didn't want Laura to have to watch this kitten die. He'd dealt with it often enough, but the idea of her seeing that didn't feel right. Especially not while she carried her own baby. He rubbed gently but firmly and watched for any sign of life.

"There. She's breathing," Cade said, grinning at Laura, who stood by his side closely watching every move he made.

"It's a girl?" she asked.

This got a big laugh from Cade. "Actually, I have no idea. If you're really good, you can make a pretty good guess with a newborn kitten, but it's really just a guess. We'll be able to tell in about four weeks."

"So, we need completely gender-neutral names?" Laura asked as he placed the last kitten at its mother's teat to nurse, and then sat back down to allow Laura to slide down next to him.

They leaned back against the wall of the tack room and watched the kittens nurse.

"I guess we do. Spot?"

Laura laughed. "For which one? None of them are really spotted. Besides, that sounds like a boy's name."

Cade pointed to the orange kitten. "O."

Laura pointed to the black kitten. "B?" Cade laughed and nodded before pointing to the kitten that now looked grayer as its fur dried. "G," he said.

Laura finished, pointing to the calico kitten. "Cal. We can call it Cal if it turns out to be a boy and Callie if she turns out to be a girl."

Cade smiled and nodded to the mother. "What about the mother cat? Can't keep calling her Mama Cat all her life."

"Hope," Laura said, looking at the cat that licked her kittens as they nursed. "Her name is Hope."

Cade watched Laura as she turned toward him and couldn't resist any longer. She looked...peaceful. Like she'd finally given in to the idea that it was safe to want more in her life.

He lowered his head to hers, pausing just the slightest bit to let her stop him if she wanted to. He didn't know how he'd stop this now, but if she wanted him to, he'd find a way. He held his mouth a scant half inch from hers, letting the tension stretch between them, before finally closing the distance completely and touching his mouth to hers.

Cade brushed her lips with his, the barest touch. Just a whisper of a kiss, but that whisper sent arousal screaming through his body. His hand threaded through Laura's hair and pulled her closer as he deepened the kiss. For one second, his heart froze while he waited to see if she would pull away or kiss him back.

CHAPTER TWENTY-FOUR

L aura thought for a split second she might be
dreaming. That maybe, because she'd imagined Cade
kissing her, pulling her into him like this so many times...her
mind had finally snapped and tricked her into believing it
was happening.

But the feel of his mouth, so soft, but strong at the same
time couldn't be denied. He was strong in a way Patrick had
never been. It was a strength that would hold her and
protect her, but she knew this man would never harm her.

Laura melted into Cade's arms, and when he pulled
back and let his mouth glide slowly back and forth on hers,
shivers raced through her. Her lips tingled from the slight
touch and her whole body felt as if it might burst. If this was
a dream, it wasn't one she ever wanted to wake up from.
Laura felt her whole body respond to Cade, coming to life
under the heated pressure of his now demanding kiss. A kiss
that stole the breath from her body and made her believe in
possibilities.

Meeeeaaaaaaaoooowww! came a somewhat twisted

yowl from the mother cat, breaking the moment and bringing breathless laughter from both Cade and Laura.

"What was that?" Laura asked, turning to Hope. "Are you kicking us out, Hope?"

Meeeaaawww, came a shorter, more satisfied meow, as if Laura had guessed correctly.

Cade pulled Laura up beside him. "I should get you home. It's late," he said, taking her hand in his as they walked out of the tack room. Red followed on their heels and hopped into the truck and Cade drove them to the main house.

All Laura could think about on the drive was that she didn't want the night to end. She didn't want to lose this feeling ever again. She wanted to fly high on the utter happiness she was floating on right now. She didn't want to wake up to uncertainty and doubt the next morning.

When Cade kissed her goodnight on the porch, she let herself sink into the thrill that rushed through her at his touch, at the feel of his hands on her arms.

But, it wasn't enough.

It was over all too soon and she was alone, walking up the stairs to her room.

"THIS ISN'T GETTING US ANYWHERE," Paul said, kicking at a bottle in the parking lot by the tire of their rented sedan.

"We've only checked two of the towns. There's still Evadale and Evers. Besides, Alec Hall is paying for this wild-goose chase, so what do you care?" Mark asked.

Paul glanced away, and Mark knew right off the bat his partner was hiding something. Paul had never really mastered the art of a poker face.

"What the hell, Paul? What didn't you tell me?" Mark asked.

"When I talked to Hall, he said he wanted us to chase down every lead, but he also said he expected results from this or we're done."

"Damn, Paul. So you all but guaranteed we'd get results down here? Even if we find the doctor, we have no way of knowing if Laura's with him. He could really be on vacation for all we know. What the hell were you thinking?"

"I was thinking I didn't really have a choice. What was I supposed to tell him? I don't know if you've noticed, but people who tell Alec Hall 'no' don't always walk away in one piece. At least this way, if we have to deliver bad news, we're a few states away. We can run before he gets someone down here to deal with us," Paul said, kicking the bottle again. This time it hit the concrete wall of the gas station and sent green glass flying.

Mark paced for a few minutes, trying to figure out which town to head to next, and how much time Alec would give them before he sent someone looking for them—or looking to replace them. And the kind of replacement Hall would have in mind wouldn't simply be a pink slip. The man usually dealt in the kind of replacement that meant an unmarked grave off the side of a highway in some desolate part of the country. Why the hell had they gotten involved with a man like Hall?

"Call your contact at the police department back home. See if they've heard anything on Laura's whereabouts. Maybe we'll catch a break," Mark said and then waited while Paul made the call.

Paul gestured for the map after talking for a few minutes. "Where was that?" he asked into the phone while Mark laid the map out on the hood of the car for him. Paul scanned the map and grinned pointing at Evers. "Thanks. I owe you one, man."

He hung up and turned to Mark. "A sheriff reported speaking to Laura Kensington. Said he had no grounds to bring her in. She was unharmed, didn't seem to be a danger to herself or anyone else and didn't want to go home. He said she was on her way out of town. Thing is, his jurisdiction just happens to have Evers, Texas smack in the middle of it."

"Let's get over there and get this done. I'm ready to be finished with Alec Hall," Mark said, jogging around to the driver's side door.

CHAPTER TWENTY-FIVE

"Do you think I can learn to ride a horse?"

Laura and Cade were leaning on the rails of one of the pastures, watching some of the newly retired horses graze in the morning sun.

Cade wrapped an arm around Laura's waist. "I think you can learn to do anything you want. Although, we may need to wait until after you have the baby for the horses. I guess we can ask Doc what he thinks."

Laura smiled and patted her still fairly flat belly. There was the slightest rounding under her hand. "I know. I can wait. I just mean someday."

"I like hearing you talk about someday here at the ranch. It's much better than that talk about running and leaving all the time," Cade said and he pressed his mouth to Laura's neck, bringing a sigh from her as she leaned into him.

When he pulled back, though, he found Laura frowning.

"What's that look for?"

Laura twisted her mouth up in the pouty little way she

sometimes did when she didn't want to tell him something. Cade put his hands on her waist and lifted her onto a flat section of the top rail of the paddock.

"What's up? Why the look?"

"Can I ask you something?" Laura asked.

"Anything."

"Why would you want to get involved with me? I mean, I'm having another man's baby. Doesn't that seem like a bad time for you to want to start something?"

Cade frowned at her. "I guess I don't think of it the same way you do. The baby is just part of you. You're a package deal. It's no different than me getting involved with you if you were a single mom," he said. "It seems to me, we need to be careful about the baby's feelings until we're sure where this is going, but we have several months for us to figure that out before the baby is in the picture. But, as for me wanting the baby if you and I decide we want a life together? That's not even an issue. It's your baby, Laura. Of course, I would want to raise it with you, to love it as my own."

Laura didn't answer, but it was clear the gears of her brain hadn't stopped grinding. She was chewing on something.

"You gonna tell me what else you're thinking about?" Cade asked, his hands rubbing up and down her thighs.

"What if the baby is like him? What if it's a boy and..." She swallowed and couldn't seem to finish her thought, but Cade knew where she was headed. He shook his head before looking her dead in the eye.

"This baby has you in him as much as he has his father's genes. And, he or she will be raised by you, loved and taught by you. That's what will matter."

Laura didn't respond but her features softened, like she might believe a bit of what he was saying.

Cade gave up trying to get her to talk. She'd talk more when she was ready. He pulled her down off the rail and into his arms, lowering his head to capture her lips. So soft, always so ready for him, melding to his mouth...as if her lips were the perfect match to his. Yup. He could definitely wait for her to be ready to talk.

Cade pulled Laura down in the grass, settling her so she straddled his lap. He wrapped his arms around her, loving the smile that stretched across her face as much as he loved the way her body fit to his, molded to him.

"Let's just focus on being together now. Let's forget about the past, stop worrying about the future, and just be here together. Now."

Laura smiled and leaned down, gently kissing his mouth, tracing the seam of his lips with her tongue. He'd first pulled her onto his lap like this the other day, thinking she might need to be in control when they kissed, after what she'd been through with Patrick. He doubted Patrick had ever allowed Laura to take such a position with him. As it turned out, Laura did like the position. And, so did Cade. She was sexy as hell straddling him and taking what she wanted from him.

Her sighs went straight to his groin as he moved his mouth to her neck and kissed her throat, nipping gently at the soft skin. He traced her jaw line with his teeth and let his thumbs brush the soft nipples of her breasts. She rocked against him in response and his cock swelled. Everything in him was screaming to plunge into her body fast and hard, with all he had.

But, he couldn't do that. He couldn't take what he wanted. They were taking things slowly, making sure she was ready for this after all she'd been through, but it took every damn bit of control he had. He gritted his teeth as her hands wandered his body, setting him on fire with every touch.

The woman turned him on in ways he had never imagined any woman could. His erection pressed against his jeans, and he wanted nothing more than to delve into her core over and over until they both found the release they needed, but he'd be damned if he'd rush her. He never wanted to make a misstep and see fear in her face or feel her tense in his arms. So, he shoved aside his urge to possess her and let her set the pace, let her take the lead.

And, damned if she wasn't erotic as hell while she did it.

CHAPTER TWENTY-SIX

Cade came up beside Laura as she put Red's food dish down for breakfast and slipped his hand into hers. Laura loved the feel of his fingers threaded through hers. It was a feeling worth keeping, worth fighting for, and she smiled up at him.

"Let's go on a date tonight. We can go somewhere nice for dinner. Maybe drive over to the city?" he suggested.

Laura shook her head, making his face fall.

"No? You don't want to go on a date?"

"I don't want to go to a fancy restaurant. I want to get pizza and go to the movies," Laura said with a smile.

"Ah. Let me guess? Going to a movie was considered beneath you? Patrick never took you to the movies?"

"Nope. No pizza, no movies. Only five star for us. I used to go to the movies sometimes during the day, but we never went as a couple. I miss just being normal, you know. I want normal," Laura smiled up at him, rising up on her tip-toes.

Cade dropped a kiss on Laura's lips, then pulled back to

look at her again. "Then normal's what you'll get. I'll see what's playing. What are you doing the rest of the day?"

"Your mom and I are making pies for the Strawberry Festival. She said it's a pretty big deal around here."

That brought a burst of laughter from Cade. "Yeah, you could say that. They shut down the whole town and block off all the roads. There are a bunch of artists that have galleries in town so they set up shows, and there are booths that sell pies, candles, crafts—you name it. Mom and her friends sell pies at a booth and then put the money toward buying Christmas presents for families in need."

Laura knitted her brows. "So, exactly how many pies will I be baking this afternoon?"

Cade's smile was downright mischievous. "Oh, I'm sure it won't be too many. You'll be fine."

LAURA WATCHED as a seemingly endless number of women flooded May's kitchen. Tables were set up in the living room where some of the women assembled boxes for the pies, and others dusted the tables with flour and set out rolling pins to roll out dough for the crusts. Another group of women were hulling and slicing strawberries at the kitchen table.

All of the women said hello to Laura when they came in, as if she were simply one of the group, as if they'd known her for years.

"Don't worry, no one's going to bite you. We're all quite nice, really," said a tiny woman whose white hair had a slightly pink tinge to it, and stood a good four inches above her head in a teased style that had Laura clamping her lips together to keep from giggling.

"Um," Laura said as the woman pushed a bowl of strawberries and a knife in front of her and pulled her down to sit next to her at the table.

"I'm Haddie. Hadeline Gertrude Gillman to be exact, but everyone calls me Haddie," she said with a smile at Laura as she nodded toward the bowl and the knife.

Laura picked up the knife and began hulling the berries and putting them in the larger bowls in the center of the table. "I'm Laura," she said.

"We know that," said another woman sitting across from her. She had beautiful black hair and striking blue eyes in a young face. "There's not a person in the county that doesn't know who you are. I'm Ashley Walker. Ignore anything inappropriate that Haddie says. She's a little eccentric and frankly, she doesn't have all her marbles anymore. Though inhibition and social graces seem to have abandoned her, we all love her anyway."

Much to Laura's surprise, Haddie smiled, wide and gleefully. "Thank you, dear. I love you all, too," she said, not seeming the least bit offended by Ashley's assessment.

"Very tactful, Ashley," said a woman on the other side of Haddie. She leaned forward and looked down the table at Laura. "Ashley has no excuse for her lack of tact. She's got all her faculties and she still says whatever she wants."

"That's my sister, Cora. She's the good little girl in the family. I'm not," said Ashley and Laura laughed as she watched Ashley stick her tongue out at her sister, despite the fact that she appeared to be in her late twenties.

"You're sisters?" Laura asked, looking from one to the other. Cora had dark skin and dark brown eyes. Her features were nothing like Ashley's pale skin and blue eyes. Even though they both had dark hair, they looked nothing alike.

Cora answered first, jumping in to speak over Ashley who looked like she was winding up to answer. "We're adopted. We have three other siblings we look nothing like, either. That'd be our brothers, Sam and Nathan, and another sister, Emma. You'll meet them at the Strawberry Festival."

Haddie chose that moment to chime back in and prove Ashley had been right about her lack of social graces and inhibition. "Did that witch, Martha Kensington, know what her son was doing to you? Did she know he was beating you?"

The loud hum of conversation in both the kitchen and living room came to a screeching halt, and Laura looked around frantically for May who was headed toward her from the living room. Before May got there, and before Laura could formulate any sort of response, Haddie continued.

"I figured it out one night when you showed up on the television set with that high-necked dress on. *Limelight Magazine* had just done a big article on you and your classic sense of style. They even had a picture in the spread of the dress you planned to wear at a gala fundraiser that week-end. The night of the gala, I watched you walking down the red carpet on that news show that always covers all the stars, and you weren't wearing that beautiful dress." She looked around the table at everyone, as though she expected them to tell her the name of the show she was referring to, but everyone simply stared back, silent as mannequins.

"Anyway, there you were in this high-necked wool monstrosity, and I knew—he was hitting you." She finished with such an air of authority, Laura couldn't utter a sound. Her throat simply seemed to close up.

"Oh, for heaven's sake, Haddie. It was a dress. And,

never mind that anyway. No one wants to talk about Laura's past. We want to know about her present, about you and Cade," Ashley said, turning to Laura. "I heard he was holding your hand in town the other day. Are you two going at it like bunnies out in the barn?"

"Ashley! I swear you and Haddie are both ridiculous! Leave Laura alone," Cora said.

"Can she have sex? She's pregnant," came one of the disembodied voices from the living room. Laura's face burned red as another voice answered, confirming that, yes, it was safe for a pregnant woman to have sex. She began to wonder if she could slide down under the table, crawl through the legs of the other women, and somehow make a break for the door without anyone noticing. She didn't know which topic was worse. Her past abuse, her current relationship with Cade, or the status of her sexual activity and whether it was doctor-approved or not.

"I wouldn't mind knowing what's going on with her and Cade. That boy's been alone since Lacey left. We were beginning to think she'd screwed with his head so much, he'd never find love again," said one of the women who now filled the doorway between the kitchen and the living room as women pressed into the kitchen to hear the conversation.

Laura's head was spinning, and just when she was about to put her table-crawling plan into action to save what was left of her dignity, she processed what the last woman had said.

"Who is Lacey?" she asked, turning to May who had made it over to her and now stood by her side. If it were possible for the room to grow even quieter, it just had.

"For heaven's sake, you all ought to be ashamed of your-selves. Can't you let Laura just enjoy a day of baking? Maybe she would have liked meeting all of you. Now we'll be lucky if we can convince her not to cross the street when she sees one of you coming," May said as she placed a hand on Laura's shoulder. "Heathens, all of you, that's what you are. Gossiping heathens."

"Who is Lacey?" Laura asked again, looking around the table this time.

Nobody said anything. They all looked at each other until Ashley shrugged her shoulders. "I'll tell her if you all won't. She was Cade's girlfriend for three years. Everyone thought they would get married. Well, it turned out he'd been trying to break up with her for about the last six months they were together. Every time he tried, she told him she'd kill herself without him. He eventually told her he couldn't stay with her because he didn't love her, and she needed to get help if she was thinking about hurting herself. Cade told her father that he should get her some help, but her dad thought Lacey was just being melodramatic."

"Cade came home and found her in his place two days later. She had broken in and taken a bunch of pills then lay down in his bed," someone from the other room said.

Laura looked up at May, eyes wide. May's expression was pained, but sympathetic as she squeezed Laura's shoulder.

"She lived. He got there in time and called an ambulance. She was checked into the hospital and then spent a few months in a treatment facility. She lives with her mom now in Austin, and only visits her father here from time to time," May said.

"Cade blamed himself," Cora said. "It was awful. Even though everyone told Cade he'd done the right thing, that he couldn't have let her keep holding him hostage that way, he wasn't the same for a long time after that. I don't think he's dated anyone since then, has he, May?"

Laura couldn't even begin to process what that meant. And if this story was true, why would he date Laura after all this time and with her history? Why date someone with so many issues, so much baggage? Shouldn't he want a nice, normal woman with a nice, normal life—and past?

"All right, that's enough, ladies. Back to work. We've got one hundred pies to make," May said, clapping her hands together. She squeezed Laura's shoulder then began issuing orders fast enough that no one had time to question Laura, much less continue the conversation about Lacey.

It was only after the pie making had resumed its conveyor-belt-like pace that Haddie leaned over and answered the questions swimming through Laura's head. "He saves people and animals, honey. Haven't you noticed? He likes saving anyone he thinks needs it. Always has."

Laura pasted a smile on her face, but her mind was racing. She'd been such an idiot. How could she not have seen that? Of course, that's why Cade was drawn to her. Haddie was right. He tries to save. It's what he does. She'd watched him with the animals he loved. They were broken in some way; all of them. And, he saved them. Took them in and saved them.

And, it made perfect sense that he'd want to save poor, helpless Laura, too.

CADE HAD a hard time focusing on his work all afternoon. He didn't want to wait even a few hours for his date with Laura. He'd seen the pie women leave about thirty minutes earlier as he'd been heading up the stairs to his apartment above the barn. He showered and then dressed in jeans and a button-down shirt before walking up to the main house to pick up Laura.

"Hey, Cade. Laura's waiting for you inside," Josh said as he pushed May in her wheelchair down one of the paths leading from the house.

"Thanks, guys. Going for a walk?" he asked as he took the steps two at a time.

"You bet. Heading out to catch the sunset. It's going to be a beauty today," Josh said, one hand on May's shoulder.

"See you guys later." Cade walked through the front door. If he'd been paying more attention, he would have noticed his mother was unusually quiet. That she'd been looking at him with troubled eyes. That might have tipped him off about what was to come.

As soon as he saw Laura sitting at the kitchen table, he knew something was wrong. She appeared to be waiting for him, but she didn't look at all like she planned to go out with him.

Laura raised her eyes when Cade entered the kitchen and immediately wished she'd taken the coward's way out and left him a note. He looked so concerned for her, so worried that something might be wrong. *Of course, he did.* But, what would happen when she learned to stand on her own two feet? Would he want her then? And would she ever be able to stand on her own if she had him taking care of her all the time?

"Hey. Laura, are you okay? Do you feel all right?" Cade asked, coming over to kneel down in front of her chair.

"Yes, I'm fine, Cade. It's just...I don't think I can do this."

"Go out? That's fine. We can stay in if you want. We can watch a movie here," Cade offered and tried to take her hand. Laura pulled back, hating to see the confusion on his face.

Laura shook her head. "No, I don't think I can do this," she said, gesturing from Cade to herself. "Us. I just can't do this, Cade."

Cade studied her with those eyes that could see right through her. "What happened between this morning and this afternoon? Everything was fine this morning. What changed your mind?"

"It just isn't what I want right now, Cade. I want to focus on myself and my baby right now, not try to lean on someone else. I know you want to save me, but I don't need saving. I don't want to be saved."

"What are you talking about? I don't want to save you. I want to date you." Cade stopped and narrowed his eyes at her as if he understood suddenly. Laura stilled as the air around them became heavy and tense. She wished she were anywhere but here. Anyplace where she wouldn't have to see the hurt in his face.

"They told you about Lacey, didn't they? They told you all about Lacey and their theory that I was trying to save her."

Cade crossed the room. "Damn it, Laura. I'm not trying to save you. What happened with Lacey happened because she was sick. And yeah, I stayed with her longer than I should have because I was afraid she'd hurt herself, but that doesn't mean I'm running around looking for other women to save. I don't care what the women of this town told you, you're nothing like Lacey. You're a hell of a lot stronger than she ever was."

Laura stood, her arms wrapped around her middle. And at that moment she realized something she hadn't been ready to admit. If she did go through with this with Cade and he lost interest when she no longer needed him, she wouldn't be able to handle that loss. She might have been strong enough to handle what her father had done to her, what Patrick had put her through, the loss of her brother. But, she wasn't strong enough to love Cade and lose him. She needed out. Now.

"You're overreacting, Laura. I'm not trying to save you."

"You ordered a commercial greenhouse for me for heaven's sake! You want to talk about overreacting?" She shook her head. "I'm sorry, Cade. But, I just can't date you," she said and turned and walked upstairs.

CHAPTER TWENTY-SEVEN

Laura sat at the kitchen table the following morning, hoping she'd done the right thing. She and Cade had done the morning chores at the stable together, but they hadn't talked any more than they'd needed to during the routine. He would usually come up to breakfast with her at the main house, but he'd gone back to his apartment over the barn for breakfast instead.

"I think I'll go sit on the front porch with this for a while," Josh said lifting his coffee mug and leaving behind Laura, May, and the uncomfortable silence that had settled among them.

Laura stood and began carrying dishes to the sink, then ran the water to warm it.

"Are you going to tell me what happened?" May asked, and Laura wanted to laugh. Or cry. She wasn't sure which one. The last thing she wanted to do was talk to May about her relationship with Cade.

She shrugged. "Nothing. We just decided it wasn't a good time to start dating."

"*Hmmm.* You're probably right about that. You have a lot going on, a lot to figure out," May said.

Laura rinsed the last dish and shut off the water, ignoring the pang she felt in her chest when May agreed it wasn't a good idea to date Cade. She took a deep breath and dried her hands. This was what she'd wanted. She had wanted to end the relationship, to nip it in the bud before Cade realized he only cared about her because she needed him. Before she was attached and it was too late to protect herself.

Laura didn't say anything as May sipped her tea and watched her. A few minutes later, May put her teacup in the sink and went to leave the room, but turned back just as abruptly as she'd left.

"You know, though, Laura. I could be wrong. It might just be the perfect time to let someone in. It might be the perfect time to let someone support you and be with you. It takes a lot of strength and courage to lean on someone else, to let them help hold you up when you think you might fall down. To take a risk on something like that. Sometimes leaning on someone else is the strongest thing you can do."

CHAPTER TWENTY-EIGHT

"Your talents are wasted here, gorgeous," Paul said, gracing the waitress with a smile that usually got him everything he wanted. She took the bait, of course, smiling back at him with what she must have thought was a sexy, come-hither smile. Two Sisters' Diner was smack in the middle of Evers, Texas and Mark and Paul had learned that people liked to chat with newcomers in small-town diners.

The waitress's efforts to capture his interest were interrupted by a very bright head of red hair and a disembodied voice that must have gone with the head. That head seemed to bob as the voice spoke.

"It's not her talent. All she does is deliver the food and pour the coffee. I'm the one does all the cooking here."

The waitress rolled her eyes. "She likes to think people come for the food, but it's the coffee. And, *I'm* the one that makes the coffee. My own special blend I mix from five different roasts." She smiled her leering grin again. "I'm Gina. That's just my sister, Tina."

Paul held in a laugh and raised his coffee mug. "It is really great coffee," he whispered, with a wink, milking her flirtatious nature for all it was worth. He was ready to get this job over with and he had a feeling this lady could help him. Working at the diner in town, she'd likely know everything that happened in this town and everyone who came through it.

"Everyone knows it's the coffee that keeps people coming back to a restaurant," Mark agreed.

"So," Gina asked, "what brings two gorgeous men like you to our town? You visiting family? Couldn't keep away from the hottest hot spot this side of Dallas? What is it?" she asked with a grin and a flirty flick of her very wide hip.

Mark and Paul both laughed, but it was Mark who answered. "Nah. We're on our way to Austin to see some friends, but we heard an old friend of ours was visiting out here. We thought we'd try to stop by and see him on the way."

"Huh. That would make three visitors all at once if your friend's here. That's more than we're likely to get the rest of the year," said Gina.

"Well, we struck out. We thought we'd be able to get in touch with him, but it turns out he's not answering the phone and we've got to keep moving," Paul said.

And, she fell for it.

"Who's your friend? Maybe I know him?"

"Josh Samuels." Paul saw the flicker in her eye as soon as he said the name. Honestly, she wasn't very good at hiding it. "He's a doctor. We worked together at a hospital up in Connecticut, but we moved on to another facility. We were hoping to catch up with him. He's a good guy." Paul finished the spiel but he could see she was gearing up for denial.

Gina pursed her lips and shook her head. "Never heard of him. And, I usually know most people that come to town.

Everyone passes under this coffee pot at one time or another. If anyone'd know him, it'd be me."

She was working too hard at the denial. Paul thought about asking about Laura, but a slight shake of Mark's head warned him not to. Mark was right. If they let the waitress think they were leaving right away, she might not raise any alarms. If they pressed by asking about Laura, she might just run right on out and tell Josh and Laura they were searching for them. The last thing they wanted to do was push Laura further underground at this point.

"Well, it was worth a shot," Mark said and pulled two tens out of his wallet and tossed them on the table. "We've got to get moving anyway. We're due in Austin this evening."

"Well now, you boys have a good visit in Austin," she said, all smiles again as they headed for the door.

Mark and Paul walked out of the diner and crossed the road to where they'd parked their car.

"I don't think I've ever seen anyone downshift so fast in my life," Mark said.

"Yup. She knows exactly who the doctor is and probably knows who Laura is, too. We can lay low for a few days, see if we can find out anything. Maybe check into a hotel and see if we can get anything out of the staff?"

Mark didn't seem to be paying any attention to Paul. He was staring at a large truck idling in front of Jansen's Feed and Grain. There were sheets of glass strapped onto special racks, and the side of the truck read Barrett's Commercial Greenhouses in big lettering.

"Thinking of buying yourself a greenhouse?" Paul asked, the sarcastic edge in his tone plain.

Mark cocked his head as they watched a man from

Jansen's talk to the driver of the truck, gesturing down the road as if giving directions.

"Didn't Alec say Laura had a huge greenhouse in her backyard? That she spent a lot of her time in it?" Mark asked.

Paul shrugged. "Yeah, but could it really be this easy?"

"Got nothing better to do than follow a greenhouse. We don't have any other leads, and we have to get something before Alec Hall decides we're not worth paying anymore."

Paul dropped the keys to the rental car into Mark's hand. "Lead the way."

CHAPTER TWENTY-NINE

Laura stayed back far enough behind the curtain of the living room window that she wouldn't be in plain sight as the car pulled up the drive. The truck carrying the greenhouse Cade had ordered arrived moments before, and there were two men setting it up at Cade's direction in one of the fields. After telling Cade she didn't want a relationship with him, watching him take delivery of the greenhouse and oversee its setup made Laura feel like a complete jerk.

But, she reminded herself, she hadn't told him to order the greenhouse. In fact, he hadn't even asked her. He'd just gone ahead doing what he thought was best for her at the time. And hadn't she had enough of that from the men in her life?

Laura watched the car until she recognized the jet-black hair of the woman she'd met the day before. Ashley something-or-other. The one with all the adopted siblings and no apparent desire to screen anything that came out of her mouth. Laura surprised herself with a genuine smile. She was happy to see the woman who didn't seem to feel the need to walk on tip-toes around Laura.

She walked through the kitchen and stepped out onto the front porch just as Ashley opened her car door.

"Christmas come a little early this year?" Ashley asked, tilting her head to the monstrosity being assembled in the field.

Laura rolled her eyes. "You could say that, I guess."

Ashley reached back into her car and pulled out two to-go cups of coffee and passed one to Laura when she walked down the steps of the house to greet Ashley.

"Yours is decaf."

"Thanks," Laura said and took the coffee from Ashley, giving her a quizzical look.

Ashley rolled her eyes. "I know. You're wondering what I'm doing here. My sister said I needed to come out and make sure we didn't do too much damage yesterday. She's picturing you shaken and shell-shocked from the encounter with the women of Evers," she said, exaggerating the emphasis on the women of Evers as if naming a mythical creature or feared monster.

"But she didn't feel the need to come check on me herself? Maybe she thought you'd handle things with more tact and grace than she could?" Laura asked, getting a laugh from Ashley. It felt really good to chat with another woman as if she were a friend. Laura hadn't had this kind of friendship in so long, she'd forgotten how powerful it could be.

"Yes, that's exactly it. That and the fact that she had to work all day."

"I was just headed to the barn to check on the kittens. Do you want to come? They're adorable," Laura said with a grin that said she knew kittens might not be up Ashley's alley.

"Oh yeah. How can I pass up kittens?" Ashley's tone said "no," but she started walking with Laura toward the barn.

"So, any fallout from your day making pies with the women?" Ashley asked as they walked.

Laura clamped down on her lips and didn't answer. How do you answer that when the fallout had been, well...pretty big.

"Oh, no. That good, huh? What happened?" Ashley asked.

Laura lifted a shoulder. "I just realized I wasn't really ready to jump into anything right now. Any relationship, I mean—"

Ashley stopped walking and looked at her but didn't say anything. Laura tried to ignore the look and continue walking, but it was clear her new friend wasn't going to move on. What was it with the people in this town? It was as if they just expected you to share everything with them right off the bat. And, for some insane reason, Laura seemed powerless to resist them.

"I just realized he was trying to save me, you know? It's what he does. He saves and rescues, but I don't want to be rescued. I want to be with him because he wants to be with me, not because he thinks I need him," she said, and they began walking again.

They reached the barn where Laura pushed open one of the double doors. Red hung back in the shadows, watching Ashley warily.

"It's all right, girl. She's rude and obnoxious, but she won't hurt you," Laura said to Red, smiling at Ashley as she said that.

"That's not true at all. I fry dogs and eat them with

biscuits and gravy for breakfast," Ashley said, addressing Red but smiling too. Red's tail wagged a little.

"Gross!" Laura laughed at Ashley's breakfast joke and walked to the tack room to look over the half door at Hope and her kittens.

"Oh look. Snacks!" Ashley said, looking over the door.

"You're terrible."

"I know." Ashley looked completely unrepentant. "So, are you sticking around for a while, or are you going to run again?"

Laura turned to look at her new friend, and she felt certain Ashley also knew about running.

"Yeah, yeah," Ashley said, reading her thoughts. "I've been a runner, too. When I got to Evers, my mom—who was my sixth foster mom at the time—told me she thought it might be a good idea to just sit tight for a bit and see what happened. She said it so simply, like that was all there was to it. If I just sat tight, things would be fine. I thought she was bat-guts crazy at the time, but she was right. She and my dad were the first people to love me just for me, to take care of me because they wanted to, not because they had to. It turned out, Evers is a pretty good place to be."

Laura unlatched the door to the tack room and refilled Hope's food bowl. The kittens' eyes weren't open yet, and their ears were still tucked tightly against their heads, but they knew she was there. They mewed and turned tiny heads toward her. Laura rubbed their soft heads with one finger at a time, taking turns from kitten to kitten as their protective mom, newly named "Hope," looked on with great suspicion in her gaze.

"Shane is helping me get ready for a court battle with the Kensingtons, so there's no reason to keep running." Laura stood and left the room, latching the door behind her.

Red fell into step behind the women as they left the barn and walked back toward the house. "And Cade is, well, he's building great big greenhouses for me."

"Do you want to know what I think? Wait, of course you do. I'm brilliant and I know what I'm talking about. Of course you want to hear what I have to say."

Laura smiled at Ashley. "Of course I do. You're brilliant and you know what you're talking about."

"If you're staying, just wait awhile on Cade. He may really want to be with you, not just save you. And, if that's the case, he'll still want that in a month or two when you're a little more sure about what you're doing, and you're feeling less like a woman everyone wants to save and more like a woman who's in charge of her own destiny, for once."

"Destiny, huh?" Laura asked. They stopped and watched the progress of the greenhouse as the panels of glass were placed along one wall.

"I might not be sensitive and lovey dovey and all that good stuff, but I'm spiritual. People find Evers just when they need it. And Cade's not going anywhere. Besides," Ashley said, looking out where Cade stood, "I have a feeling that man's worth waiting for. Tell me, did his kisses make you want to drag him off to the nearest bed, or did you just faint right smack where you stood?"

Laura gaped, but that didn't seem to faze Ashley one bit.

"Oh please, don't tell me you weren't tempted to tear the shirt off his back a time or two. That boy can melt panties with a single glance," Ashley said.

Cade turned and looked at Ashley and Laura as if he'd heard every word, even though he was twenty yards away. Laura felt the heat rush to her cheeks and Ashley only laughed harder at that.

When the laughter stopped though, Laura had one more question for her unlikely friend. "How do you know that this time wouldn't be like before? Did you know your parents were different when you stopped running?"

Ashley held her gaze with those impossibly blue eyes. "Did I know they wouldn't hit me this time? That no one would show up in my bedroom? No. I didn't. But sometimes you just have to take that chance. Sometimes, you just can't let the past rule you. Sometimes, you just have to let it go."

MARK CUT BACK through the field and out to the road where Paul was waiting for him. They'd followed the greenhouse delivery truck to a ranch twenty minutes outside of town, and then driven past it a ways before Mark got out and cut across fields and through sparse trees to see if he could spot Laura or the doctor.

Mark placed the high-powered binoculars he was carrying on the floor of the car as he climbed in the passenger seat.

"We got her." He described the two women he'd seen walking from the house to the barn. "She cut her hair and it's darker now, but it's definitely her."

Paul headed down the road a bit while Mark called Alec and reported in. The hunt for Laura Kensington was over.

CHAPTER THIRTY

A lec watched Justin out of the corner of his eye. They were on a private jet Justin had chartered as soon as the private detectives had called to report they'd found Laura. It had been crap luck that Justin was with Alec when the PIs called and he'd picked up on the fact that they'd tracked down Laura. Well, no, not crap luck. Justin had been haunting Alec almost day and night on his new quest to find Laura and liberate her, to tell her she was free to raise the baby without any interference from his mother.

Alec had tried to convince Justin that Alec should go get her alone, but Justin couldn't be dissuaded.

Justin sipped bourbon on the rocks as the jet carried them to some small Texas town with a landing strip in the Hill Country. Mark and Paul were staked out watching the ranch to be sure Laura didn't slip away before Justin and Alec arrived. Alec knew he'd need to find a way to convince Justin to let him talk to Laura alone first. Then, he needed to find a way to keep her quiet for good without anyone being the wiser about his true motives. He didn't have a clue how he'd do either of those things, but he'd come up with a way. He hadn't gotten where he was in life without being damned resourceful.

The attendant stepped into the cabin. "Gentlemen, we'll be landing shortly. Can I get you anything else before we arrive?" she asked, her smile polite and solicitous.

"No, thank you," Alec said. When she left the cabin, he turned to Justin. "It's an hours' drive from the private airport to Evers. I've got a car waiting for us."

Justin only nodded as he drained the rest of his drink and then sat back and closed his eyes. He was just as quiet on the drive to Evers, but as soon as they met up with the private investigators, it was clear Justin intended to take over the show. He grilled the investigators about what they'd seen, who Laura was with, where she was. The group stood down the road from the ranch that sheltered Laura, and Justin was ready to drive right up her driveway and try to talk to her. Alec had only minutes to try to see Laura alone so he could get what he needed and take care of her.

"Listen, Justin, I think it might be better for you to let me go in first. If she sees you, she might just think you're here to take your mother's side in this, or worse yet, that you might hit her like Patrick did." Alec knew he'd hit a weak spot with that suggestion. Justin visibly winced at the mention of Patrick hitting Laura, so Alec took advantage and pushed on. "We don't want to frighten her into running again. If I go in alone, maybe I can let her know you're here to help, that you know what happened with Patrick, and you want to make sure your mom can't hurt her. She's less likely to be frightened by me."

Justin looked from Alec to the ranch and back again. "All right. I'll hang back and let you go in first."

"Good. Mark, Paul, you guys drive us up to the bottom of the driveway and then wait there. I'll walk up and see her then wave to you guys when she's ready to see you, Justin. If she does run, be prepared to trail her." He leveled a look at Mark that he hoped he would interpret correctly since Alec couldn't be as blunt as he'd like to be with Justin listening in. "Don't lose her."

~

CADE SLOWED Cayenne's Pride to a walk. He rode the fence line along the western edge of their property helping José check for spots that might need repair. It was something he did from time to time to help their friend and just to get out on his horse more often. Cayenne's rehab was going so well Cade was having a hard time holding him back, making sure he didn't hurt himself in his eagerness to run again. But this week he'd started letting the horse run, and it felt great to be out on the powerful creature's back as he worked.

The landscape on the ranch never ceased to calm him, and after Laura's decision to end what had barely begun between them, he needed something to settle him. But this wasn't settling him in the least today. In fact, the further away from the barn and house he rode, the tenser he became. Something wasn't sitting right for him today and the urge to turn back toward Laura, to stay close to her, seemed ever-present.

Cade's phone rang—the ringtone indicated Shane was calling him. He dropped the reins over the horn of his saddle and let Cayenne amble at a slower pace.

"Hey, Shane, what's up?"

"Are you with Laura?" Shane asked without saying hello.

The hair on Cade's neck stood up and he turned

Cayenne back toward the barn. "No. I'm riding the fence line. She's at the barn."

"It's probably nothing, but I just saw Tina and Gina. Two men were asking about Doc in the diner yesterday. They said they were old friends of his who wanted to visit, but the girls pretended not to know who he was. The guys said they were leaving town, on their way to Austin, so they could already be gone, but I just thought you should stick closer to her for a few days to be safe."

Cade grunted a response and disconnected the call before urging Cayenne into a gallop. He prayed he wasn't pushing the horse too hard, too fast, but he needed to get back to Laura. He shouldn't have ignored the feelings of unease he'd had since yesterday. Even if Laura didn't want to be with him, he had to be close enough to watch her and make sure no one came onto the property without him knowing about it. He should have done what he'd promised and taken care of her, watched over her. If he'd just screwed up and put Laura at risk he'd never forgive himself. He lowered himself over Cayenne's neck and urged the horse toward home.

CHAPTER THIRTY-ONE

Laura filled the water bowl for Hope and placed it on the floor next to the cat's bed. She held her hand still for a minute below Hope's chin, and waited to see if Hope might let her get in a little scratch. The cat lowered her nose and sniffed for a second and Laura used the edge of her hand to rub at the side of Hope's face. The cat held still for the petting but appeared torn about the interaction.

Laura remembered Cade telling her he always backed off if he wasn't sure an animal wanted to engage with him. She dropped her hand and whispered goodbye, then stood and slipped from the room.

Red stood outside the tack room door and whimpered.

"All right, just for a bit," Laura said and opened the door to let Red into the room with the kittens. Red had started checking on the kittens several times a day, despite Hope's yowling objections. It was pretty adorable how the fearful dog seemed to have taken on the job of protecting the kittens as though she somehow thought they were hers. Laura watched over the half door as Red lay quietly near the litter. She couldn't help but wonder how Red would be with her baby when it arrived. She had a feeling she would be gentle and protective, and as dedicated to a human baby as she appeared to be to the kittens.

As Laura watched, Red suddenly rose to her feet, tension radiating through every muscle of her tough little body. She spun toward Laura, hair prickled along her spine, a low growl coming from deep within her throat.

"Red?" Laura asked, unsure why the dog had turned on her that way. Had she done something to frighten her? And, then she felt it. She wasn't alone in the barn. Laura didn't know if it was a slight noise she'd heard or just a thickening of the air around her somehow, but she knew clear as day someone was with her. Red hadn't turned on Laura. She'd turned on whoever had intruded into the sanctuary of the stables.

"Hello, Laura."

She spun when she heard the voice behind her, then panicked as she realized Alec Hall stood in the center aisle of the barn. How on earth had he found her? Why was he here? Was he coming after the baby or was he here because of whatever mess Patrick had gotten himself into before he died? It suddenly dawned on Laura, maybe it had been Alec who had put that look of fear on Patrick's face. Maybe whatever was on the USB drive hidden in her kitchen had something to do with her husband's former business partner.

"I'm not going back," she said, her back pressed against the door to the tack room.

Alec gave a wry smile. "I have no intention of letting you go back. In fact, I plan to make sure you don't ever go back. But first, I need to know what Patrick gave you before he died. Where are you hiding the evidence, Laura?"

That answered that question. Laura tried to think but she was frozen. She had to figure out a way to convince Alec she didn't know what he meant. She needed to delay so she could get to safety. Laura silently cursed herself for not telling Cade about the USB drive. She should have told him. Together, they could have figured out how to handle it. Maybe they could have gone to Sheriff Davies and had him contact the local police to get the drive from her house in Connecticut. But should haves and could haves weren't going to help her now.

"What evidence, Alec? What do you want from me?" Laura looked around her as she spoke and tried to figure out if there was anything she could use as a weapon. Anything she could hit him with or throw at him. She had no delusions that she could really hurt him. He was much stronger and larger than she was. But she might be able to throw him off balance long enough to run. If she could get up the stairs to Cade's apartment over the stables, she could lock the door and call for help.

The Jeep. Get to the Jeep, Laura. She could almost hear Cade's voice in her ear as she remembered the running plan he and Shane had set up for her. She had begun to think she would never have to use it, and she certainly never thought she would have to run because Alec Hall came looking for something he thought she had.

"Don't even think about running, Laura," Alec said, pulling a gun from behind his back. "I've got people waiting outside if you try to run. Now, let's talk about that evidence."

Laura knew if she told him the truth—that Patrick would never have confided in her—she would be useless to Alec alive. She needed to find a way to string him along until help arrived or she figured out a way to escape.

"Let me tell you how this is going to go. You're going to give me what I want, every damn piece of evidence that idiot husband of yours ever collected. Do that, and I let you go. If you don't, I'll tell everyone I walked in here to try to talk you into seeing Justin to talk about the baby. You pulled a gun on me, we struggled, and the gun went off." He shook his head. "I tried to save you. Did my best, with the baby and all, you know. But, I couldn't save you."

Before Laura could answer, she heard footsteps approaching. She didn't process right away that it was Justin Kensington.

"What the hell are you doing, Alec? What is this?" Justin asked from behind Alec, his voice filled with accusation, making it clear he'd heard what Alec said to Laura.

The next few seconds moved in slow motion. As Laura watched in horror, Alec spun and shot Justin. She didn't stop to think, didn't worry about the fact that this was one of the people she'd been running from. Her only instinct was to see if she could help him. She ran to Justin where he fell and tried to stop the bleeding.

She thought she might be screaming, but she wasn't even sure.

"Get up. Laura. I don't have time to screw around now," Alec said. "That shot's going to bring people running."

The horses were out in their pastures, but Laura could hear Red barking and growling from inside the tack room. She tried to remember if May and Josh were home to call for help. Surely they would have heard the gunshot....

But no, they had gone out earlier this morning. They wouldn't be home for a few hours. Cade was out on the ranch, possibly miles away. He'd left on Cayenne and hadn't said when he'd be back. Laura was alone.

She crouched next to Justin and felt for a pulse. It wasn't strong, but it was still there. Justin was still alive. Laura thought quickly and turned to stand, putting her body between his prone form and Alec. If she could let him think Justin was dead, maybe he wouldn't shoot him again and Justin would have a shot at surviving this.

"You killed him."

"No, I didn't, Laura. You did. You pulled a gun and shot him when he tried to talk you into coming home."

Laura felt sick to her stomach. Her mind whirred as she tried to come up with a way out of this, to get help for Justin before he bled out— and help for herself. Before she could think of what to say, she saw something move out of the corner of her eye.

The blurred form was so fast, Laura didn't know what it was at first. But then it hit her. *Red*. Red had jumped the tack room door and was on top of Alec, teeth clamped on his arm as the man screamed in pain. The gun fell from his hand and skidded to a stop at Laura's feet.

She froze for a split second, watching the way Red pinned Alec. But then she heard Cade's instructions in her head. *Get to the Jeep and run.* She picked up the gun and headed for the Jeep, running flat out for safety.

"Red, come! Red!" she called out as she ran. Laura made it to the Jeep, grabbed the keys from under the seat and gunned the engine as Red jumped into the passenger seat. Dust rose behind them, and she started for the dirt road leading away from her ranch, away from the first place she'd ever wanted to call home.

≈

CADE HAD Cayenne running flat out when he heard the shot, but somehow the horse dug deeper and gave him more. It didn't hurt to have a racehorse under you when you needed one, and apparently, the hock had healed well enough for Cayenne to race when Cade needed him to. As the barn came into view, he could see the Jeep tearing down the dirt driveway, kicking up a cloud of dust. Another car was headed up the drive, trying to block her way.

Cade cursed and was tempted to close his eyes as Laura veered off into one of the white rail fences that lined the drive. She must have kept her foot on the floor though, because she blew right through the fence and crossed the field, then came out onto the road on the other side, blowing through the fence there too.

Laura turned the Jeep right, away from town and out toward the highway. As Cade watched, the car that had tried to intercept Laura turned and tried to head across the field after her. Cade turned Cayenne and reached behind him for the rifle he always kept strapped to his saddle when he was out on the ranch. It wasn't unheard of to run into a wild animal and Cade never rode without his rifle.

He hadn't worked with Cayenne on loud noises at all, and had no idea how the horse would react to Cade firing a gun from his back. Racehorses heard a lot of loud noises, so it was possible Cayenne would be all right with this. Then again, he might not. Cade sank into his seat as Cayenne charged after the two cars. The horse drew parallel to the cars along the road, the vehicle following Laura gaining on her with every passing yard. Cade said a quick prayer, raised the gun, and fired.

Cayenne held steady on the first shot, but it went wide. The second found its mark, taking out the back wheel of the car, and it careened to a stop.

Laura kept driving, just as Cade knew she had to. She needed to get to safety. He wanted to pull her back, though. Back where he could protect her from whatever was happening. But, he couldn't. Laura was gone.

CHAPTER THIRTY-TWO

C ade hadn't been surprised to see Shane pull in behind the sheriff and the ambulance, and he couldn't say he was sorry to see him. It wouldn't hurt to have his brother with him through all of this. A man identifying himself as Alec Hall, Laura's husband's former business partner, claimed he and Justin arrived to try to talk to Laura and she pulled a gun on them. He said she shot Justin, told Red to attack him, and then took off in the Jeep.

Cade could barely control the rage building in him as he listened to the story. Justin Kensington was being airlifted to the closest hospital. He was unconscious, so questioning him about what had happened was out of the question. Cade hadn't missed the surprised look on Alec Hall's face when the paramedics rolled Justin out on a stretcher.

He'd covered it quickly by saying he had thought his friend was dead and he was relieved to hear he wasn't, but Cade saw through that. Whatever this man was up to, he wasn't happy to know Justin Kensington might live. Hall had been spouting about cash and a fake identity he'd found hidden back in Connecticut. He was ranting about Laura not being what she seemed. Cade had been able to explain the cash and ID to the sheriff, but that didn't help matters much.

Cade and Shane now stood with Sheriff John Davies, who had finished questioning everyone present. "My hands are tied, guys. Their statements all match. I can't hold them without anything more. If you had seen what happened, Cade, it'd be a different story, but until we either find Laura, or Justin Kensington wakes up and tells us what happened, I've got nothing to hold these guys on. I can take them down to the station to get their statements, but I can't keep them there long."

Cade cursed under his breath.

"I have to put out an ATL alert on Laura," John went on quietly.

Shane looked at Cade and translated. "Attempt-to-Locate."

"I'll make sure it's clear she's just a potential witness to an incident. I just don't have a choice right now, Cade. This is an attempted-murder investigation now, and if Justin Kensington doesn't make it, we're looking at manslaughter, at best."

Cade couldn't believe what he was hearing. He wanted to haul off and hit his friend, but he also knew this wasn't John's fault. John didn't have a choice. Cade just knew he needed to get to Laura before Alec Hall tracked her down again. He hoped she would be at the first meeting spot on the list he and Shane had made for her in two days. After the way they left things, he wasn't entirely confident Laura would show up. And that... Hell, that would just about kill him.

CADE WATCHED the front door of Baird Diner in Searcy, Arkansas from the window of his motel room across the street. He'd gotten into town the night before and slept a few hours, but most of the time he'd been in the window watching for any sign of Laura. He wondered if she'd been holed up in the motel like him or if she could be sleeping in the Jeep. He assumed Red was with her since no one had seen the dog since Alec and Justin had shown up on the ranch, so she might be camping out in the car with his dog. He hoped like hell Red was keeping her safe.

At ten minutes to noon, Cade grabbed his duffel bag and left the motel. He tossed his bag in the back seat and pulled his car over to the diner, careful to park off to one side. He had no idea how he'd even begin to look for Laura if she didn't show up here or at the other locations on the list. He guessed he'd have to find his own investigators if she didn't show up at any of the meeting points as planned. But tracking her down wouldn't be easy at this point.

After ten of the longest minutes of his life, Cade saw the Jeep come down the street. Laura slowed a little ways down from the diner as if she were watching to see if anyone waited for her. She pulled into the lot and parked, then got out of the Jeep. Red sat waiting in the passenger seat, scanning the lot with the vigilance of a sentry assigned to watch duty.

Cade opened his car door and whistled. Red's head came up and she and Laura both turned his way. The relief Cade felt when he saw the look on Laura's face couldn't have been greater. She smiled at him, and his heart damn near exploded in his chest. She was here and she looked happy to see him. He closed the distance between them and pulled her into his arms.

"I was so afraid you wouldn't be here," he said, the words coming out muffled as he buried his face in her hair, nuzzling as he took a deep breath, reveling in her scent, the feel of her safe in his arms. Red leapt out of the truck and circled them, then stood with her body pressed against their legs. Cade wanted to get Laura out of there, but he needed just a minute more before they moved. Moving meant pulling his arms away from her, and he wasn't ready to let her go again.

Laura clung to him as though she needed him as much as he needed her. "Alec shot Justin," she said into Cade's chest. "Red saved me. She jumped the door to the tack room and saved me."

"I know, honey. Justin's in critical condition. He's still unconscious. They operated but he's in a coma. It's a waiting game right now to see if he'll come out of it," Cade said.

She pulled back and looked up into his eyes. He could almost see the internal struggle going on. She rose slowly on tiptoes and pressed her lips to his, and that was all the permission he needed. Cade pulled her tight and took over the kiss, delving into her mouth to taste what he'd thought he'd never have again. She tasted of sweetness and honey and all things good and innocent in the world. He lost himself in the feel of her, in the knowledge that maybe they'd have a future together after all. That maybe she'd let him in.

Someone nearby cleared their throat and Cade pushed Laura behind him, ready to fight to keep from ever being separated from her again. It was nothing threatening. An older gentleman with laughing eyes watched them as he entered the diner. Cade took Laura by the hand.

"Do you have anything you need to get from the Jeep?" he asked. She was carrying the backpack he'd put in the Jeep for her a week ago. He'd packed her some clothing and a little money to tide her over until she got to the bus station for the money Shane had left her. She shook her head.

"Did you get to the bus station?"

"Yes," she said and pulled the backpack around to her front and touched the small zipper pocket on the side. "I got the money Shane left. I've been staying in a motel in the next town over. The night clerk was a dog lover. She looked the other way while I snuck Red in at night."

"Good. Come on," Cade said and pulled her toward his car. "I don't want to stay here any longer than we need to. We'll leave the Jeep here and go in my car."

He realized he was dragging a pregnant woman away from a diner and wondered if she needed to eat. "Have you eaten? Do we need to get you food first?" he asked looking around the lot to be sure Alec Hall or the PIs weren't closing in, even though he knew they hadn't followed him. The chances of them tracing her to that location so quickly were slim.

"I ate before I came just in case I had to run again," Laura said and his heart flipped. He hated the thought of her having to run again—even if he was with her this time.

Cade nodded and opened the door to let Red jump in the back while Laura climbed in front.

"I think we should drive for a few hours before we find a place to stay so we're nowhere near the first meeting point," Cade said as he got in and started the car. "We need to lay low for a while. Alec and the two private investigators said you were the one who shot Justin. Right now, John Davies has nothing else to go on since it will only be your word against theirs and they couldn't find the gun at the scene."

"I have the gun," Laura said, looking down at the backpack between her feet. "Can't they test for gunshot residue or something? You see that all the time on TV." Laura turned and rubbed Red's head. Red looked happy to have her people back together again. She lay with her head between the two seats, eyes closed as Laura scratched her between the eyes.

"They did, but his story covered that. He says you pulled the gun and he grabbed for it and was wrestling with you when you shot Justin, so he had residue on his hands from that. John's calling in some favors with a forensic specialist back in New York where he worked before coming here. He's trying to find out if anything about the pattern of the residue or the amount of residue or anything like that can prove he's lying, but I have no idea what the answer to that will be. For all I know, they won't be able to tell."

Laura didn't say anything for a long time. "How long do you think I'll need to hide?"

Cade threaded his fingers through hers. "*We* need to hide until I can get ahold of John and tell him your side of the story and see if he's got any new information and what he recommends. He'll tell us we have to come in, but if it looks as if we'd only be coming in to let him arrest you, I'll just politely decline his invitation until he finds some evidence to clear you." Cade lifted her fingers to his lips and kissed the back of them; the relief at having her back safely almost overwhelmed him.

"There's something else we need to tell John," Laura said and there was something troubling in the undercurrent to her words. Cade glanced at her and saw fear in her eyes.

"What is it, Laura?" he asked, squeezing her hand.

"It's my fault Justin got hurt." She seemed to be fighting to get the words out, and Cade stayed quiet, waiting for her to collect herself.

"Before Patrick died, he hid a USB drive in our kitchen. I've never seen him look frightened before, but whatever was on it had him scared. Almost panicked. I didn't dare touch it while he was still alive. And, then after...I never got a chance to. The press were at the house. But, I should have told you, or called in an anonymous tip or something. I should have told someone there was something else going on. That's what Alec is after."

"You couldn't have known that, Laura. And you can't take what Patrick did on yourself. That fault lies with him."

Laura was quiet for a long time, looking out the window as he drove. Cade waited, giving her time. A long while later she turned sideways and rested her head on the headrest, looking at him.

"I think I like being saved by you, Cade Bishop," she whispered.

CHAPTER THIRTY-THREE

Cade let Laura sleep for several hours as he drove west, crossing through states in no particular direction. They were in Kansas when he finally pulled into a state park. They might have to show identification to get camping passes, but he doubted the investigators would look to see if anyone was checking into campgrounds under Laura's name. He hoped to avoid using her name altogether, but that depended on how strict the staff at the campsite was. Some took careful track of names and required ID and others didn't.

Since Laura was asleep when they arrived, the ranger at the gate accepted Cade's word that she was his wife—a statement that felt oddly good to say—and let them in without identification from her. Cade paid cash and chose a remote spot on the campsite map when given a choice of sites. Laura began to wake as he steered the car down the dirt road that led to the site. They would have been better off in his Jeep, but since Laura had left in the Jeep, the description and license plate were included in the alert that had gone out to law enforcement all over the country. They couldn't use the Jeep, so they were stuck with May's Mazda.

"Where are we?" Laura asked, lifting her head and looking around.

"Kansas."

Laura looked at him for a minute before breaking into laughter. She turned to Red. "He brought us to Kansas, Red. Do you see the irony in that or is it just me?"

Red looked confused but Cade laughed at Laura. It felt really good to see her laugh again. "We're camping. I packed a tent and extra bedrolls so you won't be too uncomfortable on the ground. I can sleep in the car if you want." He shot her a look from across the car as he pulled to a stop in the little space for a car next to their campsite. He didn't want her to feel pressured to share a tent with him, or to feel like he was pushing for more than she might be ready to give. He desperately wanted to make love to her, but knew he might need to wait a long time for her to feel comfortable with that after all she'd been through.

Laura shook her head. "I don't want to be alone."

The campsite was nothing more than a tiny clearing big enough to pitch a tent and not much else, but there was a little creek within walking distance through the woods that would be a pretty distraction.

Cade nodded and began gathering their things. He pitched the tent while Laura let Red out of the car. Most likely, there was a rule against having a dog off leash, but Cade hadn't thought to bring a leash for Red. He watched as Red went off into the edge of the woods to go to the bathroom, but the dog never took her eyes off them and she didn't stray far. She was back by Laura's side within minutes.

"I'll put up the tent, and then we can drive into town

and get dinner. There are granola bars in that bag if you need something in the meantime," Cade said, pointing to his duffel.

He suddenly didn't know what to say to Laura. What he wanted to do was find a nice hotel room somewhere with her, not have her sleeping on the ground out in the woods.

She was just as quiet. He'd give anything to know what she was thinking.

Laura ate a granola bar while Cade pitched their tent. She watched as he tossed the bedrolls and sleeping bags in it for later. He popped the trunk of the car again and pulled out the canister of food he'd packed for Red, who immediately showed up by his side, ready to eat. Cade knelt down to hug the dog, and the dog pressed into him.

He owed this dog so much for keeping Laura safe. Alec had said Red attacked him, unprovoked, but Cade didn't buy that for a minute. This just wasn't a dog that would do that. She plain didn't have it in her. For Red to gather the nerve to attack, she had to feel she was either being threatened or Laura was.

"Thank you, girl," Cade whispered.

THEIR DINNER WAS fast and simple. They had burgers at a roadside place, where it appeared no one looked too closely at Laura. Cade thought one man watched them for a while, but when the man looked elsewhere, decided he was probably paranoid. They'd returned to the campsite and walked to the creek to sit for a bit. There wasn't exactly a whole lot you could do when you were hiding out in the woods, trying to make sure no one spotted you.

Cade had called John, and the news wasn't any better

than it had been when he'd left. Justin Kensington was in stable condition, but he was temporarily being kept in a medically induced coma. The doctors didn't say how long he'd be kept like that. He'd relayed the news about the USB drive along with Laura's instructions on where to find it and her permission to allow a local police officer to enter her home.

"Was John mad at you when you told him you weren't bringing me home?" Laura asked as they settled by the creek. Cade sat on the ground with his back against a tree and pulled her down into his lap, looping his arms around her. He wasn't going to let her get away again. She belonged in his arms.

"No. He knew I didn't have a choice, just like I know he has no choice doing what he's doing. It's his job. But, I think he'd do the same thing if he were in my shoes."

They sat and listened to the sound of the water and watched Red run and play in the stream as the sun went down.

"Tell me about Lacey," Laura said, and Cade had to fight not to stiffen. Not because he still had feelings for Lacey. He was over her and he'd gotten past what had happened. He just didn't want Laura to bolt again.

"There's not much to tell. She was sick. That's all, Laura."

She turned in his arms and looked at him. "Do you blame yourself for what she did?"

Cade shook his head. "No. I did for a while. I thought I failed her for not getting her the help she needed, but one day I realized I needed to let that go. I told her dad to get her help. And, the truth is, I couldn't just stay with her because she threatened to hurt herself. That wasn't good for either one of us. She needed more than I could give her."

Laura settled herself back against his chest. Having her there felt so damn right.

"Did she get help?" she asked.

Cade nodded and rested his head on her shoulder, breathing in the soft scent of her, nuzzling his face into the crease of her neck and listening to her breath catch in response.

"Yes. She's doing better now. Shane saw her in town recently. She's living in Austin with her mom. It sounded like she's moving on."

Cade ran his hands over Laura's belly, feeling the slight swell that was starting to form.

"You're starting to show," he whispered, and felt her shiver as his breath ran across her neck.

"Does it bother you?" Laura asked, twisting to face him. The expression on her face was like a kick to his gut. Fear of rejection, plain and simple. God, how could she not know he'd never reject her?

He shook his head. "Not one bit."

He lowered his head and kissed her, the kind of sweet long kiss he loved to get lost in with her. The kind of kiss he knew she hadn't had during her life before this.

"Take me to bed," Laura whispered against his lips. Cade pulled back and looked at her, startled that she'd ask him. She nodded and pulled his head down for another kiss, but Cade broke the contact, shaking his head.

"Not here, Laura. Not like this. You deserve better than a tent in the middle of a national park."

Laura leaned back and poked him in the chest with one finger. Hard. "Don't tell me what I deserve and what's best for me. I'm a grown woman and I know what I want," she said, emphasizing each word with another poke to his chest.

Cade flipped her to her back and covered her mouth

with his, taking her lips roughly, deeply. His tongue delved into her, tasting and demanding all at once. He let loose the pent-up passion he had for her, one hand sliding up her waist to cup her breast, then brush over the nipple. He groaned with need and pressed his rock hard erection into her. He wanted her to know what she did to him. How she drove him mad with wanting her.

He waited for her to panic. Waited for a flashback to her husband or some sign that she was unsure.

But that wasn't what he got. Laura pushed back against him, but not with her hands. She raised her hips and met his, letting him know exactly what she wanted. He pulled back and looked in her eyes, seeing nothing but passion and heat and a plea he was powerless to deny. Even if he'd wanted to, he didn't know how he could. His whole body was coiled tight and screaming to find release within the woman in his arms. He needed to make love to her. Needed to feel their bodies joined.

He lifted her and carried her back down the trail to their campsite with Red following behind. Cade set Laura down next to the tent and followed her in. He'd dreamed of making love to her for a month, and wanted nothing more than to make this what her husband should have made it for her all those years ago: perfect.

He slowly stripped each of them of their clothes, reveling in the stunning beauty of the woman who lay before him. Her body was perfection, but the look in her eyes was what went right through him. There was heat and need in her gaze, and the effect of that intensity on his body was something he'd never felt before.

He ran his hands over her soft skin, loving the way she gasped or moaned, writhing in response to every touch. Her nipples peaked beneath his tongue. He kissed each scar on her body, tracing them and creating new memories for her. Erasing those that might haunt their future. She responded so incredibly to him, her body soft and pliant as his mouth and fingers worked to show her what love should be like.

When she whispered his name, he knew what she wanted. He moved his hand to her thighs and slid his fingers between her folds. She was wet and swollen and more than ready for him. He circled her clitoris before filling her with first one finger, then two. He loved the way she pushed against him in response, riding him, driving him on with each moan and gasp. He needed to feel her surrounding him, feel her taking his body into hers. Feel her orgasm as he drove into her.

When he donned a condom and slipped inside her, the heat and the slickness of her tight channel all but overpowered him. He had to grit his teeth to keep from coming right then. But, he made himself slow down as he slid almost all the way out, before driving in again. And again and again. Over and over, she accepted him into her body, her legs wrapped around his waist, as if to pull him tighter, to bind them together.

As he looked into those eyes that had grabbed him the day she'd walked into his world, he made love to her. And, when her body tensed and she cried out his name, he felt the orgasm rip through her, and he was helpless against it. He thrust deeper, harder, and emptied himself, never wanting the feeling of loving Laura to end. Never wanting to be without her again.

Cade hugged her to him as her breathing steadied and she traced small circles over his skin with her tongue. He'd never felt more complete than he did in Laura's arms. This was where he needed to be. He knew in his heart he wanted to spend the rest of his life making her as happy as he possibly could, giving her everything she asked of him and more. He just needed to keep her safe if they were going to have a hope for that future he wanted for them together.

CHAPTER THIRTY-FOUR

Paul tried to stay calm as he dialed his contact in the Connecticut Police Department, but his hand shook ever so slightly. Mark was somehow holding it together, even as Alec held the barrel of a gun in his mouth and threatened to let Paul finish the job alone if they didn't get a lead on Laura right away. Blood trickled down Mark's jaw and Paul was sure he'd heard the crack of at least one tooth. Alec had seriously lost his head after the cops let them go. How he got the jump on Mark, Paul would never know given Mark's strength and skill, but he had. Fuck, it was likely just the fact that bat shit crazy often beat out sane in a fight.

And now Mark was on his knees, and Paul was frantically trying to get ahold of everyone he knew in law enforcement that might help them, that might give them the tiniest lead to go by.

The ticked-off look on Mark's face might even be funny if Paul wasn't so afraid he was going to see the back of his best friend's head explode any minute. Or maybe they'd get drunk and laugh about this when they got out of there.

They had laughed at more screwed-up crap than this together.

But not this time, Paul decided; if he got Mark out of this alive, he was done. They were leaving the business, or at least going a bit more legit. If Mark walked away from this, they'd move out of state to start over with new names and no more dealings with the Alec Halls of the world. They could spend their time catching cheating husbands in the act and running background checks on potential employees. Safe, simple, and a good paycheck.

"Got it. She was spotted at a restaurant in Kansas," Paul said into the phone but he looked at Alec as he said it, nodding his head. He didn't name the city or the restaurant. He had to be damned sure Alec still needed them. Alec slowly put his gun away and stepped back from Mark, whose lip was split open. Mark spat blood on the floor and Paul held his breath praying Mark wouldn't go after Alec. They just needed to hold their shit together a little longer. Just a little longer, then they could get out of this screwed up mess they'd somehow landed in.

"You have two days to track her down. If I don't have a location in two days, you better run fast and far, gentlemen."

Paul had a feeling they would need to run fast and far anyway. Alec Hall didn't look like he planned to keep any witnesses around when this was over. The look in the man's eye was no longer one of control. And a man like him out of control? Well, hell. That was a scary prospect Paul didn't want to stick around and see.

CHAPTER THIRTY-FIVE

Laura woke to Cade's arms around her, his breath warm on her cheek as he held her tightly. Nothing could have made last night more beautiful. Not a luxury hotel with champagne and rose petals. Not a soft bed instead of a tent with sleeping bags. Nothing. Cade had been patient and kind and sweet when she needed him to be, and he'd been sexy and hot and passionate when she'd needed that. He had taken her to places she'd never even dreamed of—hadn't dared to hope for before.

And, no. She hadn't had a single flashback to her time with Patrick. Patrick hadn't entered her mind the entire night. When Laura looked at Cade now, she felt hope, and that hope no longer scared her. In a way, it set her free.

She pulled out of his arms carefully, planning to sit up and sneak out of the tent to use the bathroom. As soon as she moved, she felt Cade's arms clamp down on her again, locking her in place. She laughed and nudged him, but he grunted and snuggled back into her. The action brought her body's arousal level to an instant high for him. Sadly, nature

—or the baby, she wasn't sure which—had other ideas for her at the moment.

"If you don't let me get up, I'll pee in our sleeping bag. I don't think either of us wants that," she said, smiling at him.

Cade released his hold and reached above his head to where he'd stashed toilet paper and a shovel in a corner of the tent.

"Bury it," was all he said as he handed the items to Laura and she laughed harder at the quick change in his attitude. She was surprised he didn't seem to be more of a morning person. He was always up so bright and early to work with the animals; she'd just assumed he woke up in a good mood, ready to go. Apparently not.

"Wow. I guess the honeymoon's over, huh?" Laura joked and then realized what she'd said. She blushed, but Cade just opened one eye and squinted at her.

"When I do get you on a honeymoon, it'll last a heck of a lot longer than one night, I promise. And it sure won't be in a tent with Red, a roll of toilet paper, and a shovel."

Laura could see the intense need burning in his eyes and knew he'd make good on that promise someday. She swallowed and forced herself to speak without the shaking voice she knew was threatening as she looked at him. "I like having Red with us," she said as she unzipped the tent and stepped out.

When she came back to the campsite a few minutes later, Cade was up and moving around. He pulled her into his arms for a morning kiss over her protests of morning breath and lack of toothbrushes. He laughed and released her, then pulled out a granola bar and tossed it to her and poured food into a bowl for Red. Their guard dog ate it without seeming to chew a single piece.

"Do you still have the gun you took from Alec?" Cade asked.

Laura nodded and reached into the car to pull it from her bag. She wasn't at all comfortable handling it, but she'd grabbed it before she had had time to think . Cade was quiet and calm as he showed her how to remove the safety, how to hold it, and fire it.

"I want you to keep this on you at all times, for now. If we get to a place where I think we can fire it without drawing a park ranger to us, I'll show you how to fire it. It's a lot of gun, so it's going to have a big kick and you won't have much accuracy. Chances are, you'll be knocked on your butt by the kick, so you might only get one shot in."

Laura didn't know what to say. She really didn't know how she would use that gun, even if she needed to. At her worst moments with Patrick, she wasn't sure she could have used a gun to defend herself. Aside from being scared to death at the thought of taking someone's life or injuring someone, there would have been the issue of Patrick getting it away from her and turning it on her.

"Run if you can, but if you get cornered, use the gun," Cade said.

Laura nodded and then tucked in her shirt and put the gun in her waistband like he showed her. She put another shirt on that hung down and covered the gun.

After going into town to get breakfast and a few things they could keep at the campsite for lunch and dinner, they spent the day in the woods. They watched Red race around trying to catch the chipmunks. Their loud chirps tormented the dog.

By nightfall, they'd walked back to the tent where they spent another night wrapped in each other's arms, making love slowly, almost languidly as if they both knew they could lose this at any moment.

PAUL AND MARK had decided it was time to cut their losses and take off. They'd technically finished the job for Alec by tracking Laura to a state park, and even finding the specific campground she was in. Had they not been so desperate to locate her after finding no record of her in hotels in the area where she had been sighted, they never would have thought to check the state park. A waitress at the restaurant told them a lot of visitors to the area camped at the state-run campground three miles down the road from the restaurant.

Laura Kensington and Cade Bishop were holed up in a tent at campsite number forty-nine. After texting this information to Alec Hall, Mark and Paul ditched both of their phones and the rental car that Alec's company was paying for. They picked out an old junker of a truck and hotwired it, then took off for California, intent on putting as much distance between Alec Hall and themselves as possible.

It wasn't hard to see the writing on the wall. Hall wouldn't need them much longer. They'd been overly confident in taking work from a guy like him, but they knew it was time to cut and run before things went south.

CHAPTER THIRTY-SIX

Justin Kensington's head was still thick with the effects of the coma he'd been in for days, but he was awake and functioning enough to answer the doctor's basic questions. He was surprised to see his mother standing on the other side of the bed, grilling the doctor about his prognosis. It was shocking to see her up and functioning as if there wasn't an ounce of alcohol in her system.

Images swam in Justin's head as he tried to pin down what had happened. Voices that didn't have faces talking around him. Laura shot him? That wasn't right. Why were they saying Laura shot him?

"What happened?" he croaked out, but it came out sounding all fuzzy and thick.

"You were shot, Justin. We were able to remove the bullet and the surgery went quite well, but you've been unconscious for several days. You're going to be here for a while longer, but the prognosis is good. We don't foresee any long-term ill effects," the doctor said.

"Laura?" Justin said, looking back and forth between his

mother and the doctor as the world began to come back into focus.

"The police are looking for her, Justin. They'll find her soon. She won't get away with this. She won't get away with what she did to you or your brother," his mother said, and he was shocked to see tears streaming down her face.

"What are you talking about?" Justin shook his head, but shards of pain dug in, and he had to hold himself still to ward off a wave of nausea.

"Your brother was poisoned. After Laura shot you and the police found out she had a fake identity hidden with cash, I had them exhume Patrick's body. It wasn't a heart attack. They found poison that they hadn't previously tested for, given the history of heart attacks in the family."

The doctor interjected. "It's not standard protocol to test for poisons when there isn't any reason to suspect something other than a heart attack. With the history in your family, no one questioned that he might have been murdered."

"Not Laura," Justin said. "It wasn't Laura."

His mother opened her mouth to object, but Justin raised his voice with the little strength he had. "It *wasn't* Laura. Alec Hall shot me. He was threatening Laura. Something about evidence she was hiding. Evidence Patrick had on him."

Images swam in Justin's head, but the pieces were beginning to string together into memories he could make sense of. He felt the world slipping away around him again as he gave over to the darkness that called to him, but, as if from a distance, he heard his mother ask the doctor to call Sheriff Davies.

CHAPTER THIRTY-SEVEN

Cade woke to the palest of light beginning to warm the day. Their second night in the tent had been as perfect as the first, each taking an endless amount of time to learn one another's bodies. He'd marveled at the way Laura looked when she came and the sweet sounds she made when she was coming back down to earth after an orgasm. Their day had been filled with the nervous energy of two people hiding, not knowing their next move, but their night together couldn't have been more perfect.

Even in the two nights they'd been together, he'd seen her confidence grow. He'd watched the power in her eyes when she realized his body responded to hers as much as hers did to his. Cade couldn't wait to see Laura's strength grow as she learned to let him love her for who she was, not who she'd always been told she needed to be.

He stretched and opened his eyes to find the space next to him empty. Cade laughed. He didn't think pregnant women had to pee constantly until later in the pregnancy. Laura had said that at her last appointment, her doctor said she was at a point in the pregnancy when the baby was tiny, but her uterus was tipped over and pressing right on her bladder. He believed it when he considered how often she was going to the bathroom.

A baby.

He had told Laura that they'd need to decide where their relationship was going before the birth so they weren't unfair to the baby, but Cade knew where he wanted this relationship to go. He wanted to spend his life with Laura. He hadn't ever felt like this with anyone. Not even during the time when he and Lacey had been happy together, when he'd thought he might marry her someday.

He knew he wanted forever with Laura and her baby, and as many babies as they could have down the road. He just hoped she'd be willing to go out on a limb and give marriage another try after what happened with Patrick. He hadn't flat out asked her about that, but he hoped he could convince her he was worth taking another shot on. They could take it slow if she needed to. He could wait.

Red raised her head and emitted a low, almost inaudible bark from her place beside him. It was a chuffing woof more than a bark. Cade knew that sound. It was meant to warn Cade without alerting whoever was out there that she was aware of their presence. She wouldn't have done that if it was just Laura returning to the tent.

Cade stilled as he listened. Noises around the car. Whoever it was must have come in on foot. Cade would have heard a car approaching.

Damn. Cade was stuck in the tent with no way to see who was prowling around the site, and Laura was off in the woods by herself. Was it an animal? It could just be some random person looking to see if there was anything easy to lift. But, it could also be one of the investigators or Alec himself. Cade wasn't willing to sit by and take the chance that it was just something benign. Laura could walk back into the campsite any minute.

Cade slipped his knife from beneath the stash of shoes and an extra sweatshirt he had stacked in the corner of the tent. He slowly cut the fabric on the side of the tent that faced away from the campsite until he had a large enough opening to slip through. He held the opening for Red and she crawled through to stand by his side. Cade stayed crouched low and signaled to Red to stay by his side as he moved.

Together they circled around the back of the small tent and peered into the brightening light. Cade cursed under his breath when he saw Alec looking through the car windows. He knew Alec would turn his attention to the tent as soon as he saw they weren't in the car.

Cade moved away from the campsite and circled wide around it to stay out of Alec's line of sight. No sooner had Cade gotten out of there, than Alec moved. He turned and approached the tent, looking behind him as if checking to be sure he wasn't followed.

Where was Laura? Should he send Red to find her?

Cade did his own scan of the area. He saw no sign of another vehicle. No sign that Alec had the two investigators with him. Could he have come alone?

Cade didn't want to chance it if the investigators were waiting close by to provide backup to Alec. As he watched, Alec pointed a gun at the tent and emptied what sounded like a full magazine into the tent, spraying it with bullets. He must have used a suppressor because Cade heard low pops, not loud gunshots. Had they been closer to the main circle of campgrounds, the noise might have brought someone running. Their campground was secluded enough, though, that no one else would have heard the sounds.

Alec had come prepared to kill. Whatever evidence he'd demanded from Laura back at the barn, Alec had apparently given up hope of getting it out of her. Now, he simply looked as though he wanted to get rid of Laura as quickly as he could. Cade touched Red on the shoulder and turned to move off into the woods. He cut around the other side of the site and headed for the area Laura would likely have gone to use the bathroom.

Cade heard Alec's swearing when he realized there wasn't anyone in the annihilated tent. Laura must have heard the noise, too. She was heading back toward the site when Cade intercepted her and pulled her off the trail into the shrub. His hand over her mouth, he whispered in her ear.

"You hear gunfire and you head toward it? We need to have a talk, woman."

Laura shook his hand off her mouth and looked up at him. In a completely staid voice, she said, "You were back there."

"Seriously. We're talking about this later. Do you have the gun with you?" Cade asked and held his hand out when Laura nodded. She passed him the gun and Cade turned them toward the creek. They couldn't go back to their car. They needed to get to a public location and get help. If they followed the creek, it would take them to the ranger station at the entrance to the park. With Laura ahead of him, the two walked as quietly as possible. Red pressed against Laura's leg the entire time.

They hadn't made it far when Cade heard a twig snap behind him and turned to look. Alec launched himself at Cade's legs, taking him down in a full-on tackle at the same time Red hurled herself at Alec. Hall's gun was in his hand, but he must have blown all of his bullets on the empty tent because now he hit Cade in the temple with the gun. Red was on Hall's back, but Cade heard a yelp as Alec turned and struck her with the gun, a blow hard enough to send her sprawling behind them.

Cade's head reeled as he took hit after hit. He kicked out with his legs, throwing Alec off balance. When he threw a punch that connected with Alec's jaw, Alec eased his hold for a split second and Cade rolled away.

He was stronger than Alec and bigger, but Alec had gotten a few good blows in and Cade's head was foggy and slow. He managed to yell to Laura to run, but she didn't move. Cade reached behind him for the gun at his waistband, but it wasn't there. He looked for it on the ground, but didn't have time to see much. Alec was coming at him again.

Cade spit out a curse as Alec crashed into him. He struggled to clear the murkiness in his head as he landed blows to Alec's head and shoulders. He struck out again and again, then kicked and rolled to pin Alec beneath him. Alec took advantage of the momentum and twisted into another roll, taking them both into the creek.

The water was shallow, but the icy cold must have knocked the wind out of Alec. Red was back then, and Cade saw her grab at one of Alec's legs, but Alec seemed oblivious to the pain of her jaw clamping down on him. Cade felt sickening sharp pain as his ribs cracked when Alec focused his fists on his torso.

Cade tried to see around the blood running into his eyes from the cuts on his forehead and temple. Laura was standing above them, white knuckled, the gun gripped in both hands.

"Laura, shoot!"

"I can't! I can't shoot without hitting you," she cried.

He heard the terror in her voice.

Cade was losing consciousness as Alec continued to pummel him. With all he had left in him, he threw Alec off and twisted out of the way. "Now, Laura!"

Alec lifted a rock, ready to go after Cade with it, but a shot rang out and Alec fell. Laura had hit him square in the stomach from no more than six feet away. The kick of the gunshot sent her flying back into the creek bed. Alec fell into the creek, his blood darkening the once-clear water, a look of shocked disbelief stealing over his features.

Red and Laura ran back into the stream and hauled Cade from the water. Red stood guard while Laura ran her hands gently over his battered face.

"Please be okay, please. Oh God, Cade, please." Her hands and voice shook violently as she spoke and Cade tried to answer her, but his head wouldn't stop pounding. Neither of them had a phone—they'd ditched them when they were running to ensure no one could track them. But, now Cade didn't know if he could walk out of these woods. And he wouldn't send Laura over to Alec's body to look for a phone in case Alec was still alive and conscious. He couldn't risk Laura's safety any more than he already had.

Cade put his hand on her stomach. "Baby okay?"

"Yes," she sobbed, nodding her head. "But you, Cade; I thought he was going to kill you."

"Not that easy," Cade grunted and rolled onto his side, then shoved up onto his knees. "Wait here," he implored, hoping she'd stay back.

Cade half crawled, half dragged himself to Alec. He laid his fingers on Alec's neck, but there wasn't a pulse and the red hue of the water running downstream told Cade the man had bled out quickly. Cade dug through Alec's pockets and found a phone in his chest pocket, but it was too wet to use.

He pulled himself back to Laura, who helped drag him up onto the bank of the river and sat cradling him in her arms.

"Someone will have heard the gunshots," he said and Laura finished his thought.

"A ranger will come to investigate. They'll get us out of here," she said and wiped some of the blood from his face. As Laura held him, Cade gave in to the blackness that washed over him, taking him under completely. Laura was safe.

CHAPTER THIRTY-EIGHT

L aura sat by Cade's side in the hospital watching him sleep. The nightmare was finally over. She couldn't believe Alec Hall had poisoned Patrick and shot Justin. She hadn't really liked the man, but if anyone had told her he was a murderer, she probably would have laughed.

The police in Connecticut had retrieved the USB drive from the house. It detailed years of embezzlement from Kensington-Hall Developers by Alec and also had some evidence of pay offs and bribes. Apparently, when Patrick confronted Alec, the other man decided to take advantage of the history of early heart attacks in the Kensington family.

There wasn't any sign of the private investigators that had come after Laura with Alec at the ranch. Honestly, Laura didn't care where they were. As long as they didn't come back, she just wanted to forget all of this.

Shane, Josh, and May had arrived in Kansas to be with her and Cade until he was well enough to travel home. He'd suffered a concussion and several cracked ribs, on top of bruises and contusions that Laura hoped didn't hurt as badly as they looked like they did.

Cade's eyes opened slowly, and he turned his head to look at her. Relief swept through Laura, making her weak. She'd never been as scared as she was when she'd seen Alec and Cade fighting. When it looked as if Alec was going to kill Cade, she couldn't bear the thought of life without him. At that moment, Laura believed she was about to lose everything she'd found, all over again. Everything she'd dared to hope for. And because of her, Cade had nearly been murdered....

"You okay?" he asked and winced as he tried to raise a hand to her face.

"Try not to move. You have cracked ribs. That's very painful," Laura said and sniffed, trying not to let tears come. She was well aware of the pain of cracked ribs. It wasn't pleasant.

"You're okay? The baby?" Cade's eyes flashed to her stomach.

"The baby's okay. I'm okay. May and Doc are down in the cafeteria getting a cup of coffee and Shane is outside sitting with Red." She took his hand in hers and held tight. His right hand was too swollen to hold. He would be getting a cast on that in the next few hours. "They've been taking turns sitting with her since she can't come inside, and I didn't think it was safe to leave her out in the car alone." It had killed Laura to sit outside with Red before Cade's family had arrived, but she knew he'd want Red to be safe and not feel frightened. The poor dog was traumatized enough by the whole episode. Being left alone in the parking lot would have overwhelmed her.

Cade smiled and closed his eyes, his breath returning to

the steady quiet of sleep once again. Minutes later, though, he woke again.

"Is now a good time to talk about that honeymoon? Will you take pity on me while I'm injured and agree to marry me?"

"No, I won't." Laura laughed. "But I'll let you take me on a date when we get home."

Cade nodded and closed his eyes again. She could tell he was fighting the effects of the drugs the doctors had given him. He pushed open his eyes once again and looked at her.

"I love, you, Laura. I couldn't have made it if Alec got to you."

Tears ran down Laura's face as she nodded. "He didn't get to me. I'll be right here when you get up, I promise," Laura said, thinking about the possibilities of that. Of staying with Cade forever. Laura knew in her heart that was what she wanted, and she had finally found the courage to accept what she wanted for herself, to embrace it and let herself hope and dream and believe in love.

Cade looked into her eyes. "I love you Laura. I want you in my life forever."

"Well, you do live a charmed life. I imagine your dream will come true." Laura leaned down and kissed Cade gently, careful not to hurt his swollen jaw. "I love you, Cade Bishop. I'll love you forever."

EPILOGUE

Laura looked down at the perfect tiny nose and rosebud lips of Jamie May Bishop. Her baby had been born two weeks before her due date, and only fourteen hours after Laura Kensington had become Laura Bishop in a ceremony attended by nearly every resident of Evers, Texas.

"She's incredible," she said and looked up into Cade's eyes with tears in her own.

Cade looked down at Laura, and then back to the baby neither of them seemed to be able to keep their eyes off of for long. "Just like her mama. Absolutely incredible." The awe in his voice was clear.

Cade leaned in and kissed Laura's lips, but the private moment didn't last long. May and Josh knocked on the door and entered with an armful of balloons and stuffed dolls.

"Really, you two? Did you buy out the entire gift shop?" Laura chastised.

"You bet we did, Princess," said Josh as he bent to kiss Laura's head. Josh hadn't gone back to his job in Connecticut. He had used up his vacation time and then officially retired. He and May seemed to be growing closer and closer, much to Laura's delight.

Cade and Shane were a little uneasy about the change in the relationship between a man they'd always thought of as their uncle and their mother, but when pressed, they both admitted they liked the happiness Josh brought to May's life.

May reached for the baby with a question in her eyes, but Laura didn't hesitate. "Of course, you can hold her," she said and passed over the swaddled bundle.

"Don't get used to this," May said with a smile as she looked down at the baby, who didn't bat an eye when the transfer took place. "They sleep like mad for two days, but then the honeymoon's over and you're only in for short bursts of sleep in between feedings and diapers."

May paused to look at the bundle in her arms. Cade and Laura hadn't planned a honeymoon. They knew since they were getting married so close to Laura's due date, there likely wouldn't be time for a honeymoon. They planned to take a long vacation for their first anniversary instead.

"She's beautiful, Laura. Just like her mother," May said, and Laura felt her heart swell at the love in May's voice. She would never have believed she would find the kind of love and family that now surrounded her.

A knock on the door announced new visitors. Shane poked his head in and Laura waved him in. He was followed by Justin Kensington, who had settled in Evers after checking out of the hospital himself a few months back. Laura had been hesitant when he'd come to see her after moving to town, but she valued his friendship now. He was nothing like Patrick. In fact, at times, it was hard to believe they were related. Justin had given up traveling, and was now using some of his wealth to start outreach programs for women and children in abusive homes.

Martha Kensington had been shunning the limelight recently and attempting to repair the damage done to her relationship with Justin. She had even been talking about moving to Evers to be closer to Laura and the baby. Justin was now at least speaking with her, although their relationship remained strained, but Laura wasn't sure yet that she wanted to have Martha in their lives. It would be hard to let someone who had ignored the abuse Laura had endured for so long be around her and her child now. In some ways, though, Laura thought forgiving Martha would help her heal even more than she already had.

Although Martha hadn't discussed it with either of them, Justin suspected she might have been the victim of abuse at the hands of his father. If she had, Laura hoped Martha would be strong enough one day to seek help with that and to heal.

A nurse came in and chased the visitors out and urged Laura to get a bit more rest before they checked out the following day. Cade took Jamie from his mother, letting his daughter rest in the crook of his arm as he and Laura said good-bye to everyone.

"I love you, Laura Bishop," Cade said and kissed her lips when they were finally alone with their baby.

Laura closed her eyes briefly, feeling the light touch of his love in that kiss.

Hope. Laura watched Cade and Jamie and knew it had been worth it. The risk of hoping, of dreaming of a love and a life like this one. It was all worth it in the end. To have the gift of love like this, the gift of family and friends who loved her. It was a gift and a blessing for which she would always be grateful.

SHERIFF JOHN DAVIES stepped back from the doorway. He would leave the flowers and the gift for the baby with someone at the nursing station rather than interrupt the private moment Laura and Cade were having.

Seeing the way Cade looked when he was with Laura, the happiness in his friend's face, made John wish for that for himself. Not that he was going to find that. Instead of letting his thoughts go to the last woman he'd shared a bed with, he shoved away any hope he had for a future like the one Laura and Cade had just found.

Thankfully, he couldn't dwell on any of it. The radio on his shoulder crackled to life and Berta Silvers' voice came through.

She coughed that cigarette cough and started over. "Got a call from Sheriff Bowden's neighbor. Says he's on the front lawn confused. Wearing his boxers and socks, but not much else."

His dispatcher insisted on calling Alan Bowden Sheriff Bowden even though they also gave John the title when he won the election. He didn't blame them. His predecessor had been sheriff of this town longer than John had been alive. It was a hard thing to let go of a title that had become almost a person's name.

What did bother him was the fact Alan seemed to be more and more confused lately. John couldn't write off the episodes any longer. He needed to get Alan to a doctor and probably put in a call to his daughter to let her know what was going on.

Katelyn Bowden. The fiery red head hadn't been to see her dad in over six months. She wouldn't want to hear from

John but she'd want to know what was happening with her dad. John had no choice but to call her.

He looked down to the gift and flowers in his hands before answering Berta. " On my way, Berta. On my way."

~

UP NEXT IS sexy Sheriff John Davies' story. Are you ready for him? Check it out in Promise and Protect! Grab the book here:

loriryanromance.com/book/promise-and-protect

Or keep reading to get the first chapter FREE!

~

CHAPTER ONE

WOW. Don't hold back, Dad. Tell him what you really think.

Katelyn Bowden leaned her head back against the icy tile wall of the hospital corridor and listened to her father and Sheriff John Davies argue. The hallway reeked of pine-scented cleaner, a smell that had always set her on edge.

Katelyn gritted her teeth. Her father was dying. She'd come home to be with him during his last weeks—maybe months if they were lucky—and now that she was here, he wanted to send her away. That was nothing new to Katelyn, but her cheeks heated at the thought of John hearing this from her father. Humiliation was becoming an all-too-common feeling for her lately.

"Of course I called her, Alan. You're in the *hospital*. Why wouldn't I call your only daughter and tell her to come home?" John asked and Katelyn wasn't surprised by the confusion in his voice.

Katelyn had heard her father's opinion on her coming home before, albeit a gentler version. She knew exactly what he would say. He probably hadn't ever shared his thoughts on the topic with John, though. John probably believed Katelyn stayed out of Evers, Texas—her father's hometown—by choice. People here couldn't possibly understand her relationship with her father. The only thing the people of Evers saw was a daughter who never came home. They had no idea why.

Katelyn frowned. Her father didn't *exactly* keep her at arm's length. Well, he did and he didn't. It was complicated. He was loving and caring in his own way with her. Throughout her entire childhood, he'd rarely missed one of his monthly visits to her in Austin, and as sheriff of a large portion of the Texas Hill Country, that was saying something. When he was with her, he doted on her. He simply didn't want her here, in his world. Katelyn had learned at an early age she wasn't ever going to be allowed to come home.

Her father's tone was harsh and unyielding as he spoke to John, drawing her back to the present. "You send her away, John. You tell her you made a mistake. She...she doesn't need to see me like this. I'll go see her when I'm feeling better."

Ah, a new argument. Now her father could say he didn't want her to see him in his current condition. There were some advantages to being on your deathbed, after all.

Katelyn knew if she walked in the room, her father would soften. He'd cajole and persuade instead of demand and order. He'd tell her she should be in Austin, where she'd grown up with her aunt. He'd say she needed to stay near her studio for the sake of her art, be near the gallery that sold her work.

This time was different, though. Katelyn wasn't going

back. She would tell him she already had another artist ready to sublet her studio and she planned to put her condo on the market. She would tell him it was too late to go back. She hadn't had time to pack much, but she would hire someone to pack the rest of her things and have them sent in the next week or so. Whether her father liked it or not, Katelyn was coming home to Evers.

Of course, neither John nor her father knew she had another reason for being in town. She wouldn't tell her father the whole story. He didn't need to know she'd been mortified to discover the man she'd been dating was hiding a wife and newborn infant from her. Or that her so-called friends simply shrugged when she told them and said they thought she knew. Katelyn wasn't sure whether it said more about her friends that they thought she knew but didn't care, or more about her. Why would they think she would do something like that? That she'd be that kind of person? When the call had come from John telling her how sick her father was, Katelyn had grabbed at the chance to walk away from all the mess and start over.

The door to her father's room opened with no warning and John came storming out. He pulled up short when he spotted her, and she could see the pity on his face when he realized she'd been listening to their argument.

"Katelyn, I..." He reached out a hand, but Katelyn stepped away, crossing her arms over her chest.

"Have you had an update from his doctor? Do they think I'll be able to take him home soon?" she asked, putting the conversation firmly in the realm she wanted. She wasn't about to discuss her relationship with her father with anyone—least of all John Davies.

She had started hearing about her father's Golden Boy when she was twenty-two and he'd come to work for her father, who was sheriff at the time. Her father couldn't stop talking about the man who would take over his department when he decided to retire. About the man who had become more than someone he mentored. The man who was like a son to him.

When she met John two years later on one of her rare trips to Evers, nothing John had done had been able to make it past the grudge she carried for him. By the time Katelyn met John Davies, she'd been firmly past the point of ever seeing him the way any other woman might. His golden blond hair and mesmerizing eyes might have captured most women's attention. Of course, she noticed he was tall and built like a tank. A very well-muscled, armored tank with a six-pack to die for and sinewy arms that could make a girl melt. But, she didn't respond to his natural good looks or his ready, dimpled smile. She didn't care if he flirted with her or turned on that charm that seemed to come so easily to him. Katelyn had seen John through eyes tainted with the strain of her father's desire to keep her out of his life.

She and John had continued to see one another from time to time over the years. He'd come for dinner when she visited her father, and was always open and friendly with her. If John noticed her dislike of him, he never brought it up. But, the resentment on her side remained.

Standing in the hospital corridor with him now, Katelyn was shocked to find she *wanted* to let John comfort her. She wanted to let him hold her and tell her everything would be all right, that her father would be well again, even though she knew that wasn't true. So she reverted to what she did best. Katelyn shoved her feelings and emotions down, swallowing them before they could surface to where she'd be forced to face them. She looked at John with what she hoped was a blank expression and waited for him to fill her in on her father's medical status. The faster she found out what was going on, the sooner she could see her father and get home to deal with, in private, the emotional turmoil that was threatening to take over.

"Kate," John tried again.

"Katelyn." Oh, she knew she was being unacceptably rude, but she didn't want this man's pity. Didn't want it and didn't need it. "I can go find his doctor, if you don't remember all the details."

John leveled her with one of those looks he seemed to reserve only for her. The look that said he was simply patronizing her. The look that said he could read every thought and every emotion. How she hated it when he gave her that look.

"All right," John said slowly. "Why don't we grab a cup of coffee in the cafeteria, and I'll fill you in."

Katelyn didn't move to follow him. "I'd prefer to speak here and then go see my dad, John. I'm tired. I've just driven four hours, and I want to visit with him and then get settled in at home." There was that word again. *Home.*

So absurd, really. Her father's home in Evers hadn't been her home in years. Decades, really. Not since she'd been sent away when she was four years old. Not since her mother's murder.

"Fine," John said with a clipped nod. "The cirrhosis is as advanced as they thought it was when I called you earlier. There's no reversing the damage to his liver. He's not eligible for a transplant because he's flat out told his doctors he has no intention of giving up alcohol. He's got six months, tops. Most likely, a lot less."

Katelyn swallowed and tried to keep her face an even mask, showing little emotion, but she had to glance away from John and blink back the tears that were pushing their way out. How had her father hidden this from her?

Her voice turned to a whisper, even though she tried to put the strength of the anger she was feeling behind her words. "How did this happen, John? When...?" Katelyn looked down and gathered herself before meeting John's eyes again. "Why didn't you tell me he was drinking this much? How could you let him do this?"

She saw the wave of guilt hit John's face, and she felt bad for a moment before she managed to draw up her anger again. He should have told her. If he wanted to be a son to her father so damned much, he shouldn't have stood by and let this happen.

"I'm sorry, Katelyn. At first, none of us knew it was so bad. Once we figured it out, well, there didn't seem to be any way of stopping him, and honestly, we never thought things would get so bad so quickly. The doctor thinks he may have had an underlying medical condition that caused the cirrhosis to advance faster than it would have otherwise, but they just don't know for sure, yet."

His voice trailed off as though he didn't know what else to say, and Katelyn knew John didn't have any answers for her. Her father had been forced out of office two years ago when his opponent in the election for sheriff ran a malicious campaign in a bid to win. He had claimed her father was too old to perform his duties any longer, harping on his age again and again. The campaign had gotten downright ugly and her father had eventually stepped down rather than lose. He asked John to run in his place, believing it was the better thing to do for his constituents. John was young enough and had plenty of respect in the community to win the election without breaking a sweat, but retirement had turned out to be way too hard on her father. Retiring without finding her mother's killer...well, that had been more than he could handle. At least without turning to drinking, apparently. And, drinking heavily, it seemed.

"Fine," Katelyn said, mirroring what John had said only a moment before. She didn't have much fight in her right now.

"There's more, Kate," John said quietly. He moved closer to her in the hallway and looked around them before speaking. "I didn't want to mention this on the phone, but your dad's been confused lately."

She stared at him, not understanding. "What do you mean, confused?"

"He's experiencing some dementia. They're not sure yet if it's a result of the liver disease or if it's something entirely separate like Alzheimer's, but he's having episodes."

"Episodes?" She frowned. She was so used to her father being sure of himself. Confident that he was right all the time. Much like the man standing in front of her now. John was always in control, always in charge.

Katelyn shut her eyes for a moment, trying to rein in her emotions. She would *not* cry in front of this man. She took a deep breath before opening her eyes.

"I don't understand." She couldn't picture her father confused or unsure, despite what John said. "What kind of episodes?"

"He doesn't always know who I am when I visit. Or he knows who I am, but he forgets the year. The other day, he thought he was still sheriff and I was his deputy. He thought he'd been injured and that's why he was in the hospital. He gets frustrated, angry, when he can't remember things," John said.

She nodded, feeling like she was losing the last piece of

her family. Wait, she *was* losing the last piece of her family. Her mother was gone. Her aunt, too. Now, her father. ...

"You need to be prepared, Katelyn. Some days, he may not know you," John said, his voice low and almost apologetic.

She cleared her throat and raised her chin to deflect the too-sympathetic look in his eyes and ward off the hot tears that threatened to fall. "Anything else?"

John shook his head. "No, that's it. The doctor said he'd tell us tomorrow whether they'll recommend discharging him or whether they want to keep him here longer. He said we could talk then about hospice options."

She had the bizarre realization that everyone here probably thought nothing of John Davies being involved in her father's care and any decisions that had to be made. It was clear the doctors and nurses had no problem giving him information and asking him to make decisions, federal privacy regulations be damned. Apparently, small town tradition could override even the most stringent of laws. Did they even think twice about the fact that *she* was Alan Bowden's flesh and blood while John was just...?

What was John? Surely not just someone her father worked with. But, he wasn't family either. She wouldn't accept that. And she wouldn't let the nurses and doctors act as if he were family. She'd tell them tomorrow that John did *not* have authority to make decisions or even receive private information, for that matter.

"I'll speak to them tomorrow."

John eyed her with an expression she couldn't quite read. "He'll need twenty-four-hour care if he comes home. I can help, Katelyn."

"No need. Thank you for calling me, John. I can take it from here." Katelyn turned and shoved open the door to her father's room. Time to face the man who'd sent her away twenty-four years ago and certainly wasn't happy to see her back.

JOHN SAW the flash of anger in her eyes and watched as Katelyn pushed open the door to her father's hospital room, her face set and resolute. She'd always been strong. There was determination and strength evident in everything Katelyn did. But he'd never seen her quite so angry, quite so stubborn.

He had suspected she would resist his help. He wasn't exactly high up on Katelyn's list of favorite people. But Alan Bowden had saved him years before. He'd somehow taken a man who had no reason to live, who had demons chasing him clear from New York City to Texas, and he'd brought him back to life. John owed Alan for that. He owed him everything. And he'd be damned if he'd let Katelyn shove him aside when the man who'd saved him from himself years ago lay dying in a hospital bed. She might not like him—even more now that she blamed him for letting her father drink—but she *was* going to have to deal with him.

He turned and walked down the long hallway toward the parking lot. The hospital was ten minutes outside of Evers, on the highway leading to Livingston Falls. He'd spent the whole day at the hospital, so he planned to swing by his office and check in with his deputies before heading home for the night. As John pushed through the exit door, the radio that lay on the left shoulder of his tan uniform crackled.

"Sheriff, you there?" Berta Silvers, the craggy-voiced dispatcher asked.

Roberta Silvers was most likely in her late sixties, although there was some dispute as to her actual age since she'd been celebrating her fifty-fifth birthday for at least the past ten years. Years of smoking left her sounding like a bullfrog trying to sing opera. Berta was an indispensable member of his staff, and one of a team of people who helped him run the sheriff's office in Evers. As sheriff, John had a whole host of duties, including overseeing the county correctional facility and prisoner transfers within the county. Together, everything often left him running on nothing more than fumes.

On top of it all, since Evers had always been too small to have its own police force, John was contracted to provide local law enforcement services for the town. Berta was not only his dispatcher; she was also largely responsible for keeping the local office running smoothly.

John keyed the large button on the side of his radio. "Yeah, Berta. What is it?" he asked.

"Danny wants to know if you're coming back in to the station. He picked up Trent Everman again. Boy is looped out of his gourd. Danny wants to know if he should hold him or call his father."

John uttered a curse under his breath, but by the sound of Berta's croaking laughter, she'd heard it. He settled into his cruiser before answering her. "Was he driving?"

"Nope. Walking down Lilac Street, headed toward the bar to see if they'd serve him," she said with a laugh. She and John both knew no one at Pies and Pints would serve anyone underage. The owner, Manny, wasn't a stickler about much, but he didn't serve anyone without legal ID.

"Let him sleep it off in one of the holding cells. No

reason to call his dad." That wasn't entirely true. At eighteen, Trent might no longer be a minor, but he was under the legal age for consumption of alcohol. Calling his dad wasn't an option, though.

Not only was calling a parent on an eighteen year old not an option, Trent's dad would beat him senseless for drinking again. John wanted the kid to quit, but not enough to let his dad go after him with his brand of parenting. It was probably that parenting style that had started the kid drinking in the first place. John would figure out another way to handle this situation.

He steered his car out of the hospital parking lot and onto Route 190, heading into the station to see if he could sober Trent up and talk some sense into him. Then he'd come up with a way to get the kid in to see a counselor or to join a support group or something. John sighed. He hated no-win situations, especially ones like this that had him turning his back on something illegal.

When he got there, it was clear Trent wouldn't be in any shape to talk with anyone for several hours—likely more. John left instructions with Danny to call him when the kid was sober and awake then left the station house for the night. Despite telling himself to go straight home, he pulled his patrol car to the side of the road across the street from Alan Bowden's house.

Katelyn's little car was in the driveway and the kitchen and living room lights were on. She'd made it home. John wasn't quite sure what he was doing there. He wanted to know how things had gone with her father at the hospital. He wanted to ask her how she was holding up after seeing her father lying almost unrecognizable in the cold, impersonal hospital room. It had shocked the heck out of John to see the effects of the cirrhosis, the swelling of his face and legs, the discoloration of his skin. He could only imagine what that must have done to Katelyn.

He wanted to comfort her, just as much now as he had when he'd seen her face at the hospital today. His fingers had itched, wanting to reach out and cradle her, hold her tight so her father's words wouldn't cut her so deeply. He'd known, though, she would never accept that from him. Katelyn would never allow him to comfort her.

She'd made it perfectly clear she didn't want to have much to do with him. But they would have to see each other if he was to be any help to her and her father. Which he *would* be, whether she liked it or not.

John scrubbed a hand over his forehead, trying to squeeze out the headache that had settled in behind his eyes. If today had been any indication, dealing with Kate would give him a lot of headaches over the months to come. And yet, here he sat like an idiot, wanting to go inside and make sure she was okay.

John shook his head and forced his gaze off the house as he threw the car in gear and pulled away from the curb. The last thing he should be doing is sitting in his car wondering how Katelyn was doing and if she would slam the door in his face if he approached.

Probably.

Well, Katelyn could slam all the doors she wanted. Alan needed him now. That was all that mattered.

READ the rest of Promise and Protect here:

loriryanromance.com/book/promise-and-protect

≈

THANK you to my wonderful husband for his patience and support. It's truly a wonder that you put up with me. No, really. Truly.

Thank you to Jessie Winter for her endless brain-storming and reading, to Cathy Cobb for brainstorming the plot over and over with me, and to my critique groups for reading bits and pieces and helping to shape the characters and the story.

Thank you to Patricia Thomas, Bev Harrison, Jessie Winter, and Jean Jenkins for their editing. Thank you to Patricia Parent, my final set of eyes, for cleaning up after me. Thank you to all of the friends and friends-of-friends who read the pre-release version for me. I owe you all so much.

ABOUT THE AUTHOR

Lori Ryan is a NY Times and USA Today bestselling author who writes romantic suspense, contemporary romance, and sports romance. She lives with an extremely understanding husband, three wonderful children, and two mostly-behaved dogs in Austin, Texas. It's a bit of a zoo, but she wouldn't change a thing.

Lori published her first novel in April of 2013 and hasn't looked back since then. She loves to connect with her readers.

For new release info and bonus content, join her newslettter here: loriryanromance.com/lets-keep-touch.

Follow her online:

facebook.com/loriryanromance

twitter.com/Loriryanauthor

instagram.com/loriryanauthor

Made in United States
North Haven, CT
20 June 2024

53869074R00167